MOMENTS IN TIME

A COLLECTION OF SOME OF MY FAVORITE SHORT STORIES

Miracles, angels, or just coincidence
What do you think?

MARILYN C. JOHNSON

Paperback: 978-1-64184-940-1
Ebook: 978-1-64184-941-8

Dedicated to my children, Robert, Anthony and
PoppyAnn Jessica,
and to
the memory of my dear husband, Bob.
I am so grateful for your encouragement and love.

And in memory of my dear grandson Tyreal.
Your chair is empty now but you will never
be forgotten.

TABLE OF CONTENTS

INTRODUCTION

There is a place that resides in the future of every person. Like a mirror, it reflects who you were and who you are. It is waiting to reflect who you will become. Every moment, you make choices. Each choice determines the path you will follow in the next moment. That next moment is your future. What is your choice: Generosity, selfishness? Kindness, cruelty? Loving, hating, caring? In each moment of time, what will your choice be?

I think everyone has witnessed miracles and everyone has seen angels. Some recognize them. Some see only coincidence, or look for a scientific reason. But what can you call it when something happens that cannot happen? A wrong number that wakes you to find your house is on fire. A toddler runs out into traffic and arrives, unbelievably, unhurt on the other side and says a lady helped him but no one is there. You are lost in the middle of the night on a dark, lonely road in a snow storm and suddenly headlights are behind you and a car goes around you then slows. The car doesn't stop so you follow it to a small town with an open gas station! You are safe. You pull in and get out of your car to thank that driver. But there is no car, it's gone.

MARILYN C. JOHNSON

How often do you look back at the past and think, what if? In that moment of time, what if I had done that differently or spoken differently? Would my life be changed now? Would other lives perhaps be changed?

Moments in time
What do you think?

A WORD FROM THE AUTHOR

Why did I write these stories? Because every time I picked up a pen they started jumping onto the paper. They wanted to be read so I helped them.

I have always loved books, stories of people far away or down the road. Stories where animals talked and flowers sang songs and wonderful things happened. I learned to read when I was almost four. And I think I knew even then, this is what I want to do, make stories.

My baby sister liked having someone talk to her so I did. I would sit on the swing with her on my lap and tell her stories about living on a farm far from the rest of the world. She listened attentively as we swung back and forth. (Thanks, Pat!)

My Daddy was a sharecropper. He worked on the big farm all day then came home and did any maintenance needed and worked on our vegetable garden, the biggest garden in the world (or so I thought) until it was too dark to see outside. Our tiny farm came with his job. He grew up on a farm and loved farming. We had a cow and some chickens and a wonderful dog that saved my life once. My Mom was raised in the city but embraced farm life for my dad. She worked all day long, cooking, cleaning, caring for the animals, milking the cow, mending clothes (patches on top of patches), canning anything and everything that grew and taking care of all of us, holding the family together. We were poor, no getting around that, everybody around us was poor but still we had all the necessaries, especially love.

We moved back to Minneapolis and lived close to my Grandma and all our extended family the summer before second grade. I missed the farm until I discovered the library. The library! They had books! Millions of books! And I could go there and take books off the shelf and sit at a table and read them. It was awesome! The library lady was a kind soul. She noticed me coming every day, all day. She told me I could get a library card. Then I could borrow books and take them home and read them. I immediately ran home with the paper my Mom had to sign and ran back. I remember I could hardly breathe watching her fill out my library card. When she gave it to me, she said, "Now you can borrow books." I clutched my new card, ran and grabbed three books and brought them to her desk. Would she really let me take them? She signed out the three books and I walked out the door. But I didn't go home. I sat on the library steps outside and read them. Then I went back inside and returned them and got three more. I did that all day long until I had to go home for supper carrying three books and my library card. She was the most patient person I have ever met. The next day, I came with my wagon and a lunch. I had a pillow in my wagon and I spent the day laying in my wagon reading. I did that all summer. Sometimes I had to stay home and help my Mom. But that was okay because I had three books to read to myself and over and over to the other kids and their friends. It was a glorious summer.

I always wanted to be a writer and through the years, I wrote lots of stories and poems, and song lyrics. But life got in the way. I married young, had two baby boys, and a girl. I worked as a computer programmer (that was fun!). My husband loved to travel so he crisscrossed the country with the kids and me hanging on to his coattails. He even took us to Switzerland for three years, lovely country. Somewhere in there, I wrote and directed a number of children's plays, musicals, for the Children's Christian Theatre.

And, through all those years, the short stories and poems and almost done novels accumulated in filing boxes and sat on a shelf in the closet and some were lost.

So, here we are. I hope you like these stories as much as I have enjoyed writing them.

Happy Reading!

THE NEW YEAR'S SNOWSTORM

She threw herself face down on the bed, unable to stop the gush of tears. Her striped gray cat, China, curled up on the pillow above her head, purring solicitously. Kate was so disappointed. Why am I bawling my head off over a snowstorm? But it wasn't just the storm.

This was her very first party since moving into her very first apartment three weeks ago. She had worked so hard, scrubbing and painting, covering the worn couch with colorful sheets, hanging her favorite pictures. She had done it all herself refusing any help from her parents and friends. She had a job and an apartment, and tonight, she was giving the best New Year's Eve party ever. With candles and appetizers and a new sparkling long gown, secondhand but gorgeous. Even her fingernails had cooperated, polished scarlet with no chips. She had invited all her close friends, and all had accepted. Everything was perfect. And then the snow came.

It started about noon, a few feathery flakes, beautiful. One to two inches, the weather report said. She wasn't concerned until about four. The snow had gotten worse and worse, swirling around from the increasing wind until you couldn't see across the street, and it was piling up everywhere. Then, the phone started ringing. One by one, her friends canceled. She tried to laugh with the first few calls, but by the last, she just bit her lip and said of course, she understood. It was then she had looked around at her almost-ready party and ran for the bedroom.

She sniffled loudly and turned on her side and felt something hard under her shoulder. She sat up and looked but saw nothing. She reached under the pillow and pulled out a small figure. She blinked several times to clear away the tears then looked closer at the tiny figure. It was an angel, a small carved and painted angel, with red hair, just like Mary's.

She smiled as she thought of the rowdy redhead and some of the crazy things they had done growing up next door to each other. They were inseparable until graduation when Mary went away to college and Kate got a job. *I miss you, Mary*, she thought, *I wonder how you're doing*. She jumped up, clutching the angel, China following, and dialed Mary's dorm. She waited impatiently through seven rings. "Hello?" It wasn't Mary's voice. She wasn't there. Leave a message? "No," Kate said, "No message." She hung up and looked down at the angel. The word Peace was written on the angel's banner.

Kate smiled. "Appropriate," she said to China. "Just thinking about Mary makes me feel better. She went to the kitchen, China leading the way, and hung the angel on a suction cup in the window over the sink. She looked out at the snow swirling in the darkness lighted only by the streetlight and the light from her window. She shook her head. No one could go out in this. Then, she squinted her eyes and leaned closer to the window. What was that by the fence? Was there something there? Surely not, but...

She ran to the closet and pulled her boots over her bare feet, then grabbed her coat, pulling it on as she yanked open the door and ran down the steps, hiking up her long skirt with one hand, grabbing the railing with the other, her coat open wide, slipping, almost falling, peering ahead into the darkness. Where...? There!

She lifted her boots high to get through the drifted snow, heading for the fence at the end of the sidewalk. "Lord, help me," she prayed aloud when she reached the fallen woman huddled against the fence post. Kate touched the woman's cold cheek. Her eyes were almost iced over. Kate tried to lift her, but she was too heavy. "Stand up!" she screamed. The woman moved her head groggily, then grabbed the fence post and with Kate's help, pulled herself up. She was shaking badly from the cold, and she couldn't see, but she tried to help as Kate dragged and pulled and propped her up, all the while screaming at her to walk, to move, to live. The woman was nearly unconscious and fell onto the steps. It took all Kate's strength to push and pull her up onto the porch. China scrambled to the side and watched as Kate dragged the woman into the apartment. The woman wasn't responding anymore. Kate yanked the woman's coat open and listened to her chest. She could hear her heart, and she was breathing. Kate threw off her coat and ran for blankets to cover the woman. When she got the hair dryer from the bathroom shelf, China pushed something off the shelf onto the floor. Kate picked it up. It was another angel. Its banner said Hope. Kate pushed it into her pocket.

She wiped the ice from the woman's face and aimed the blow dryer at the top of the woman's head to dry her icy wet hair. The woman opened her eyes.

"It's okay," Kate said. "You're inside now. The woman nodded. "Do you think you can walk? You should get into bed and warm up."

"Baby," the woman whispered.

"Baby?"

"Baby," she repeated. "One one six."

"One one six? This is one one six, but there's no... Oh, upstairs. You mean upstairs?"

The woman nodded. "They called me. Hurry. Baby coming."

She tried to sit up but fell back. "They need me. I—I am midwife."

"But—"

"Please." The woman grabbed Kate's arm. "Please, please tell them I'm here. I can help them." She paused. "I just need a hot drink first."

Kate nodded and ran to the kitchen. She filled a cup with hot water and rushed back. She lifted the woman's head and helped her to sip the hot water. The woman moved her legs. Kate quickly removed the snow-filled boots and wet socks. She wiped the woman's feet. They didn't look frozen, just very cold.

"Please! Go tell them."

Kate hurried out the door and ran up the stairs and banged on the door of the upstairs apartment. The door flew open, and a young man grabbed her arm and pulled her running to the bedroom. He looked terrified. A young woman lay on the bed, very pregnant and obviously in labor. "Thank God you're here! I didn't know what to do! The baby is coming!" There was fear and helplessness in his voice.

Kate had no idea what to do. The midwife would never make it up the stairs. She looked at the man's slight build. He couldn't carry her up. The two of them together couldn't. She looked back at the woman on the bed. Even with her swollen middle, she was very small. Kate smiled.

She and the man wrapped a blanket around his wife, and the two of them carried her down to Kate's bed. They put a chair next to the bed and helped the midwife to the chair. They told their names, and for the next two hours, Kate and George followed Louisa's instructions and helped bring Kerry's baby into the world.

As Louisa gently laid the newborn on his mother's chest, George kneeled by the bed, weeping and hugging his wife and new son. Louisa sank back into the chair, exhausted.

Kate glanced at the clock. It was midnight. The phone rang, and as she reached for it, China jumped down from the tall chest where she had watched the birth. Something fell next to the phone, another angel.

"Hello?" Kate said softly. She didn't want to disturb the new family.

"Happy New Year, Katy! It's Dad. We just wanted to call and say Happy New Year. We love you very much, honey."

Kate smiled. "I love you, too, Dad. Thanks for calling."

"How is your party going? I don't hear any noise."

Kate laughed. "No one made it, Dad."

"The storm?"

"Yeah."

"I'm so sorry, honey. I know how important this was to you."

"It's okay, Dad. It really is." She paused. "Daddy, do you have room at the table for one more? I'd like to come home tomorrow and be with you guys." She laughed, "If I can get through the snow."

"You will? Mom, Katy's coming home tomorrow."

Kate could hear shouting in the background. She laughed again. "I have a lot to tell you and Mom. This has been quite a night."

"Is everything okay?"

"Everything is fine. I'll tell you all about it tomorrow."

She finally hung up. Her father was a dear man, but hard to get off the phone.

The phone rang again. It was Mary. She was at the airport. She had come home for New Year's. Kate would see her tomorrow. As she hung up, Kate picked up the angel figure. Its banner said Love. Kate smiled and pressed the angel into the sleepy mother's hand. She opened her eyes for a moment and looked at it and smiled. Then she sighed, patted George's arm, and closed her eyes, the angel resting in her open hand.

Kate watched for a moment, China purring and rubbing against her leg.

"You know," she said, "I have lots of food. I'll go warm it up. We'll celebrate the new year."

In the kitchen, she filled four plates and warmed them one by one in the microwave. As each was ready, she carried it to the bedroom. Even Kerry sat up to eat. As she lifted the last plate from the microwave, something clattered on the floor. She looked down. China batted it around until it hit Kate's foot, then she sat back and looked up expectantly. It was another angel, the fourth. As Kate bent down to pick it up, China walked into the living room. Kate's eyes followed her to the torn Christmas paper and open box lying on the floor by the decorated tree. She followed the cat and bent down to look closer at the box. It had come that morning, but she hadn't opened it yet. China obviously had. On the side of the box was stamped "Contents – 4 angels". There was no card, no return address, no manufacturer information. She never did find out who it was from.

She held up the tiny angel and smiled. Its banner read Joy.

"Peace, Hope, Love, Joy." She nodded.

"Happy New Year's, China!"

THE ANTIQUE SHOP

A bell tinkled when I opened the shop door. I stepped inside then hesitated and glanced around. It was a small, hole-in-the-wall antique shop. It was dimly lit, and the twilight outside barely penetrated the grimy windows. The shop was a large, very cluttered room with furniture crowded together. Every flat surface was covered with bric-a-brac and books. The walls were filled with dark pictures of many sizes, all in dark frames. I squinted in the gloom but couldn't make out what most of the pictures were. Everything looked old, very old and dusty. The whole place smelled musty. It didn't look promising. I liked old things, but this place...

I started to step back out the door when I noticed a picture hanging on the far wall. It looked like it was framed in white wicker. A dusty light made it glow slightly. I couldn't tell where the light was coming from. I could see it was a picture of the inside of a shop with a marble-topped counter in the foreground. I didn't really care what the picture was anyway. I loved white wicker. If the frame was nice, maybe I would buy it just for the frame.

I stepped forward, and the door closed behind me. I hesitated again.

"Good evening," a soft voice broke the silence.

I jumped and abruptly turned toward the voice. I hadn't noticed the shopkeeper come in. Or maybe he was always there, and I just hadn't seen him in the gloom. "It doesn't matter," I whispered to myself as I made my way through the furniture to the back of the room where the shopkeeper stood behind a marble-topped counter, directly under the picture in the wicker frame. He smiled at me. I nodded back and looked up at the picture.

He smiled and asked if I liked the frame. I did.

"Look closer," he said.

I walked over to the wall and looked up at the picture and blinked. It looked different somehow. I saw now that a man was clearly standing behind the counter. How strange that I didn't notice that before. In fact...

I looked around the shop. The picture was of this shop. I glanced at the shopkeeper smiling at me. He was the man in the picture.

"It is magical," he said, coming from behind the counter. "Each person who looks at it sees something different. What do you see?"

"I see a picture of you in this shop," I said slowly.

"And?" His voice sounded amused.

"And... There's another person in the picture. A woman, I think. I didn't see her before. The light is very dim."

"Do you recognize the woman?"

I frowned. "She looks like me!" I stared at the picture.

"Yes, you are looking at the present, this moment. What else do you see?" He moved toward me.

"That's all." I moved to the left, away from the man. He was too close. I didn't like people to be so close. Not since John died. I was alone now. The kids were all grown, gone. They had their own lives, as they should. No one needed me anymore. I had nothing better to do than poke around in old, run-down shops looking for... What was I looking for?

I just wanted to lay down and die too. There was nothing for me anymore. I turned my head away and blinked my eyes to cover the sudden rush of tears and sniffled as quietly as I could. But he heard. His old, leathery hand touched my arm. Sympathetically, I knew, but I jerked away from him.

He was between me and the door, so I turned to study some small, very old-looking pictures on the countertop. I picked one up. A man and woman. *Husband and wife*, I thought. It reminded me of John and me. I set it down quickly and picked up another. It was a little girl in a turn-of-the-century dress sitting in a wooden cart being pulled by a much bigger girl.

"It reminds me of my sister," I said. "When we were little, I used to pull her in a wagon."

"So, it reminds you of your past?"

"We were best friends then."

"And now?"

I shook my head. "We're both so busy. I rarely see her anymore."

"Do you have a picture of her?"

I thought a moment. "No, well, wait, yes I do."

I took out the small photo album I always carried with me and set it on the counter. He picked it up and removed some of the small photos one by one and laid them on the counter, their edges overlapping in a collage. I looked at the pictures. I was so happy when they were taken.

His hand gently touched my head, and turned my face toward the wicker frame.

"Look now," he said.

I looked and caught my breath. On the counter in the picture were all my little photos.

"How… "

"This is your past," he said softly. "You were happy then. But now… you think you will never be happy again."

He leaned toward me and whispered, "But you will be happy, a little bit more each day. A little bit, a little bit, you will heal. And you will love again. And you will be loved."

He looked down at the photos and smiled as he said, "You are loved right now. See the pictures."

I looked again at the photos.

He was right. I wasn't really alone.

"Next year," he said as he overlaid the photos with others from my little album. "Next year, you can call all these people and tell them you love them. Next year, you will feel better. Next year, you will have love."

I touched my finger to my sister's picture. I traced the outline of her face. This was not an old picture. It was taken just last summer. I smiled.

His hand gently touched my head and again he turned my face toward the wicker frame.

In the frame, I saw myself looking at the photos of all the people I loved arranged in a collage on the counter, my finger touching my sister's face.

"This is your future," he said. "Next year," he added.

I stared at the wicker frame. I wanted to believe what he said. Next year maybe...

"May I buy the frame?" I asked.

"No," he replied. "But I will give you this one, so you will remember. Look at it often next year."

He took a small wicker frame from the wall, a frame I had not seen there. He gathered all my photos and laid the pile inside my little photo book then he laid the frame on top. He placed them in my hands and walked me to the door.

I heard a clock striking the hour. One, two, three times it struck and continued striking.

As I stepped outside the clock struck the twelfth time, midnight. The old man said, "Happy New Year."

He looked up, and I followed his gaze. The dark night was aglow with stars as if a mighty hand had picked up sparkling sand and flung it across the sky. I caught my breath.

"It's so beautiful," I whispered. "I haven't looked up for so long..."

I turned to the old man and said, "Happy New Year. And thank you."

As he closed the door, he smiled.

"Next year..."

I nodded, and he said, "Next year is here."

NEW BEGINNINGS

Janet and George had been living in a motel, having just arrived in town for George's new job. Things had not gone so well at George's old job. There was a girl… Janet said she would stay with him only if they moved away from there. She was surprised when George agreed.

They had gone to a realtor to ask about houses in this area because they liked this neighborhood of older houses that were nicely kept up with small yards and sidewalks. And, it wasn't too far from George's new office. The realtor had been reading a listing when they came in and got very excited when they described what they wanted. She had just received a foreclosure listing that fit the bill. No one had even seen it yet. It was a steal, and the owner had apparently died without heirs. The realtor hadn't seen it herself yet, but the pictures looked great. And it came with furnishings! They had no furniture, so that sounded good.

When they walked in the door of the house, Janet knew it was perfect. It was small and cozy and obviously had been loved. Nothing had been removed; not even family pictures. She was so excited. George was more interested in the possible value of the furnishings and what other valuables they might find, not to mention the low price of the house. But for Janet, it was a new beginning. They bought it and moved in two days before Christmas.

Janet walked around the Christmas tree that she had placed in the middle of the front window. For the past hour, while she was putting on the ornaments, passersby had been stopping on the sidewalk to wave and smile. They had just moved in yesterday, and already it felt like home. True, the furnishings had all come with the house, but still, she had rearranged a few things to make it their house and talked George into buying a tree, and she decorated the tree. George had grumbled about the foolishness of putting up a tree when tomorrow was Christmas Eve but even he smiled now.

She held the last ornament, a beautiful and apparently very old ornament, all burgundy velvet and gilt. She had found it in the box marked "Christmas" in the attic of the small house. The ornaments were all colored balls and icicles except this one. It had been carefully wrapped in cotton batting and put in a small box of its own inside the bigger box. There was a note with it that read "Give this to Billy when I die. He always loved it. Love from Grandma." The writing was difficult to read, obviously written by an unsteady elderly hand. Janet was touched by the note and saddened. Who was Billy, and why didn't he get his ornament? And why didn't anyone want all the other things left in the house? Nothing had been removed, not even clothes or linen or kitchen things.

"Your hot toddy is getting cold," George said, smiling. He sat on an overstuffed and surprisingly comfortable couch watching her hang the ornaments.

"This is the last one," she replied cheerfully.

She stood by the tree and lifted the ornament to hang it when her eye caught a movement outside the window. There was a man standing on the sidewalk staring at her. She frowned when she recognized him. She had seen him out there looking in the window before, several times. He was very thin, dressed like a bum with dirty, wrinkly clothes that didn't quite fit and a pasty face. *Probably on drugs*, she thought. He gave her the creeps.

"George," she said turning towards him, "It's that man again."

"What man?" George stood up and looked out the window. There was no one there. Still, he knew whom she meant. The man had been out there on the sidewalk looking at the house at least three times. George came to the window and put his arm around Janet. He frowned then realized she was staring at his face, his reaction, and he smiled broadly.

"Want me to hang this last one?" he asked, reaching for the ornament in her hand.

"Sure," she said, handing it to him. She went to the couch and sat down.

George hung the ornament on an upper branch. It was beautiful, and it glittered in the flickering tree lights. He went to Janet and sat down beside her putting his arm around her shoulders. She leaned into his embrace. They had an uneasy peace between them, more like a truce, he thought, a very fragile truce. He deeply regretted hurting her and wanted desperately for her to be happy again. And he wanted her to trust him again. *Time*, he thought, *it will take time*.

He glanced at the window and stiffened. Janet looked up, and her eyes got big. The man was out there again. George jumped up and ran to the door. He yanked the handle and ran out and down the steps.

"Hey," he shouted. "Who are you and what are you doing here?"

The man was young, in his early twenties. His face was pinched as though in pain. He backed away from George. He was limping. It was then George noticed the small cane on which the man was leaning.

"Who are you?" George shouted again.

The man licked his lip anxiously then whispered. "I used to live here."

"So what?" George was angry now. "You hanging around out here is scaring my wife. You get away from here and stay away!" He shouted, stepping forward, fists up.

"Wait," the man whispered. "I just wanted to see the old house again." He turned to go, then turned back.

"The velvet ornament on the tree. Would you sell it to me? I'd really like to have it."

"Get out of here! I bought this house and its contents. Everything in it belongs to me now!"

"I know," came the whispered reply. His voice was pleading. "I just wanted the ornament. That's all."

"Get out of here before I call the police!"

"Okay, okay." The man held up both hands then turned and quickly limped down the street. George watched the man walk away then went back into the house. Janet was watching from the doorway.

"What did he say? She asked closing the door. I couldn't hear him."

"He said he used to live here."

"Did he tell you his name?"

"No".

"Do you think he'll come back?" She asked.

George stared out the window then shook his head. "No, I don't think so."

Janet looked up fearfully. "What if he does come back? What if…"

"Janet," George interrupted. "Let's go to church tonight. The paper said they were having a play or something. It would be fun." She looked at him doubtfully. He smiled. "I love you," he added.

She looked into his face and slowly smiled then reached for the local newspaper. The service would begin in about an hour. They hurriedly dressed and walked to the church. It was a beautiful service with children doing a nativity scene and singing. The pastor spoke of forgiveness and helping those in need. They stayed for coffee and cookies. Several neighbors recognized them and came over to say welcome. They were glad someone was living in the house again.

Janet mentioned the ornament, and one neighbor, Ida, remembered the little boy, Billy. His parents were killed in a car accident when the boy was very small. Elizabeth, the former owner of their house, was the only relative. She raised her grandson. He was a good boy. Then something happened when he was away at college. They thought Billy got in some kind of trouble. He never came back, and Elizabeth never talked about it. They figured he was still alive because she still prayed for him. When the pastor asked for prayer requests, she always prayed the same thing, "Keep Billy safe and close to You, Lord." He had been gone several years now. It was funny he didn't show up for the funeral. But then, probably no one knew where to reach him. He sure loved his grandma. They knew that. And she sure loved him.

"Keep Billy safe and close to You, Lord," Ida repeated. "You know, it's funny, but since Elizabeth died, I've been praying that for her," Ida confided.

Several other neighbors laughed. "So have I."

"And me."

"Me, too."

They left the church feeling safe and accepted. It started snowing lightly, but the sky was still clear with one star shining brightly. This was their new beginning, and they held hands. When they came to their house, George suddenly pushed her behind him. The front door was ajar. George whispered, "There's someone in the house. Stay here. No, wait! Go to the neighbors and call the police."

He started forward, and she grabbed his arm. "Wait for the police," she whispered. He turned and tipped his head towards the neighboring house. She hurried toward it as he moved stealthily toward their front door. Just as George went in the front door, Janet saw a shadow arm reach up behind the Christmas tree, and she screamed. Jake opened the front door when he heard her scream. They saw a tussle of swinging arms in the window, and the Christmas tree tipped over. A man burst out the front door, glanced at Janet, then hurried down the street away from them. He was limping as he ran. Jake watched him for a moment then he and Ida ran with Janet to her house. George was on the floor trying to disentangle himself from the light strings, and they helped him up.

"Was it…?" Janet asked.

"It was that same guy." George was furious and frustrated. "Who is he? And what is he after?"

They called the police, and they came out. Nothing was missing. George didn't get a good look at the guy but was sure it was the bum who was watching the house earlier.

When the police left, they righted the tree then went to bed. They didn't sleep well, and in the middle of the night, they were both wide awake, so they went down to the kitchen for hot cocoa. Janet sat close to George thinking about all he had given up moving here with her: his friends and his career. He gazed at her and thought of all he had almost lost. They both prayed the same prayer, *Lord, help us to stay together*. The next morning, they slept late then sat together in their bathrobes on the couch listening to Christmas music.

They were surprised by the doorbell's chime. George opened the door. Jake and Ida stood on the little porch. Jake looked embarrassed, but Ida was determined.

"Hi, Jake. Something wrong?"

"No, it's just that…" His voice trailed off.

Ida glared at him then spoke, her voice breaking, "That man last night. We know who he is. We didn't want to get him in trouble, but—breaking in and knocking you down. We should have told you, but he used to be such a good boy and …"

"It was Billy," Jake interrupted. "It was Billy."

19

"Billy?" Janet stared at Jake and Ida. Then she slowly picked up the small ornament box laying on the end table. She took out the note. "Give this to Billy," she read.

"It's his ornament," she said softly. "This is his grandma's house." She looked around, and her gaze fell on a picture on the fireplace mantel, a picture of a young man with an elderly woman. "Is that Billy?"

Jake looked closely at the picture. He frowned then nodded. "Yes, that's him."

"We'd better get back home," Ida opened the door. "By the way, that ornament opens if you twist the top."

After they left, Janet lifted the ornament from the tree and twisted it. Nothing. George took it and twisted the other way, and the gilt top came off. A small key lay inside. George picked it up. "There's a number on it. It's a safe deposit box key. No bank name."

They looked at each other.

"Janet," George said quietly, "this house is our new beginning. If we go looking for the bank and find it… There could be a will." He paused. "We could lose the house."

Janet looked at him for a long moment and said nothing.

He took a deep breath and let it out slowly as he shook his head. "We've got to do it."

Again, she said nothing.

"Janet?" His voice sounded choked. "Will you leave me if I do this?"

Janet smiled. It was like the sun coming out. "Let's do it," she said.

They found the bank. They couldn't get to the box, of course, but the manager did tell them Billy's name and signature were on the card. If they could find Billy, he could open the box.

They went looking for Billy, asking every person they saw. They found him at the bus station boarding a Greyhound bus. He was scared when he saw George but got off the bus and went to the bank with them.

The bank manager recognized Billy and said, "Welcome back. Sorry about your grandma."

Billy thanked him. When asked where he had been all this time, he pretended not to hear.

Billy signed for and opened the box with Janet and George watching. The will was there and the deed and a pile of cash and an insurance policy. Janet and George held hands tightly and thought about the house they were losing and the boy they were helping, and both decided they had done the right thing, and God would reward them somewhere along the way.

And God did reward them.

Billy stayed at the house. They went to church together on Christmas day, then the three of them went to the cemetery to see Billy's grandma's grave. Billy buried a piece of paper under a corner of the stone, his last letter to his grandma.

Janet made dinner for them in the afternoon. Billy told them he had spent three years in prison on a drug charge. He was out now with a pardon because he saved a guard's life during a riot. His leg was broken, and his larynx was injured; that's why he whispered. George told him they would move as soon as they found another place, but he said no, they should stay here. His grandma would like that. They were good people, and it was a good house. The only thing he wanted was the ornament.

"Grandma always said it was my past and my future. Her mother brought it from somewhere in Russia. She was going to give it to my mother, but she died when I was little. Grandma said she would give it to me when I was grown so I could pass it on." He paused. "I'm going back to college after the new year. I want to do proud by my grandma. I'm going to make a new beginning to my life and do it right."

After dinner, Billy insisted on cleaning up. George and Janet stood next to the Christmas tree looking out the window.

"This is a new beginning for Billy. You think he'll make it?" he asked.

She nodded, smiling.

"We get to keep the house after all. Strange, huh?" George paused. His voice dropped to a whisper. "Janet, we can make it too, can't we?"

"Can we?" she asked.

He nodded.

She looked at him and smiled. "Yes, we can make it. This is our new beginning, too. We'll make it just fine. Together."

RICKY'S NEW YEAR

Ricky sat quietly in the center of Camp Snoopy in the Mall of America. His hands were buried in his jacket pockets. He shivered. Since he arrived in this frozen city, he was always cold. The snow and frigid temperatures were so different from his home in Juarez. It was so warm and sunny there, but here... He shivered again and pushed his hands deeper into his pockets, his shoulders hunched. He watched the people walking by, the children skipping along, holding their parent's hands; people who belonged here.

Tonight is New Years, he reminded himself morosely. He closed his eyes thinking of his family, his mother and Rosalita, his sister. They would be praying for him, wondering how he was. He missed them. His mother had not wanted him to go. But there was no work there. With his father gone, he needed to take care of his family. He wanted so to find work and be able to send for them.

He opened his eyes, blinking away a tear. He had crossed the border thirty-seven days ago at night, in the dark. He pictured the others, the young family with four children, one a new infant, the old couple holding hands, and the other young men like himself, all hoping to find a better life. He remembered the Border Patrol lights coming on all at once, all around them. He was so afraid; they all were. The women screamed and tried to run, but with little children, they were caught right away. The old couple didn't even try to run; they just kneeled down together and prayed. The young men were fast and ran hard, but they were all caught—except him. He was not on shore yet. A little girl had fallen in the water, and he pulled her out and pushed her up on shore to her mother. Ricky was still climbing out of the river when the lights came on. He dropped back into the muddy water and swam downstream until he had to come up for air. When he burst out of the water, he could hear the Border Patrol loudspeakers, but he was far enough away that they did not see him. For days he had run, hiding whenever he saw a police car or if anyone stared at him, afraid of being caught and sent back. He was still afraid. *I'll probably always be afraid*, he thought.

His friend Raul had made it across the border several times. He had always gotten caught eventually, but he learned a lot about how to hide and live and find work as an illegal. He shared what he learned with Ricky. Hide, blend in, never stand out, smile. Never act afraid, and go north, he said—so that's what Ricky did.

The further north he got, the safer Ricky felt. He even hitched rides, mostly with truckers because they didn't ask uncomfortable questions. He could speak passable English. Raul had said there were jobs in the north. The north was magic. It was where his future lay.

Now, here he was in Minnesota, the United States of America, the land of prosperity and opportunity—and police. He bent his head down and pretended to read the newspaper he always carried. Read the front page like an American, Raul had said. The police never bother anyone reading the front page. It was true. The security guard walked by, barely glancing at Ricky without stopping.

His stomach rumbled softly. He was hungry. He smiled ruefully. He was always hungry since he came across the border. The "guide" had taken most of his money. Not that he had much to start with. It just meant he had to be very careful. This was not the growing season; there were no fields filled with fruit or vegetables. He had found he could sit in fast food places a long time if he bought something. Mostly he just bought coffee and took a long time drinking it. He would stop in grocery stores and buy bread and peanut butter and make sandwiches. It was always the same, but it kept him going.

He had made a few dollars by unloading some trucks. When he started this journey, he had thought that he would have a job by now. He had asked about several jobs, but each time they wanted identification. He always pretended he had left it at home and would return. He never returned. He had to find someone who would hire him without papers. His mother always said to be honest, but how could he? It was hard living like this. If he didn't find something soon…

He sighed. He could walk around the mall until they closed, but where would he go then? It was snowing and very cold. His jacket was thin; he had no boots. He had even considered stealing a warm coat from one of the careless men who hung it up in an unwatched coat room, but he was not a thief.

He stood up, closed his eyes, and stretched. His neck was stiff. When he opened his eyes, he froze. There, three stories above him, he saw a little girl, not more than two or three years old. She was on the edge of a scaffold, part of the construction taking place on the third level. Her hand was on a crossbeam that was right next to the scaffold. There was a large angel bear sitting on the cross beam about ten feet away from the scaffold. How did she get there?

Then, he saw the open gate. She must have seen the bear through the open gate. She started pulling herself out onto the crossbeam. Even as he watched, he was praying and running toward the scaffolding. He began climbing up the side then suddenly stopped. If he saved her, he would be found out and deported. He thought of his family with all of their hopes and dreams resting on him. But the little girl…

It seemed like he thought for a very long time, deciding what to do. In reality, it was less than a second. The decision was made when he saw her. Everything in his nineteen years of living, learning, caring, and being loved made the decision. His body just willingly followed.

He reached the third level of the scaffold. He was very close to her, only about six feet away, but he would have to cross the beam to reach her. He knew he couldn't balance on the narrow beam. He was afraid to breathe, never mind speak, for fear she would turn and lose her balance. It was a miracle she hadn't already fallen.

He glanced down and wished he hadn't. It was so far away that it made him dizzy. He shook his head and kneeled down. His hands grasped the crossbeam. It was so small. People were looking up now. They saw the child. Some women screamed. The child was oblivious to everything except the angel bear.

Ricky sat down and swung his legs out over the edge, then very slowly he lowered his body out and down until he was hanging from the beam. He hung by one arm to see if he could. He could, but probably not for very long. He gulped and grabbed the beam with his free hand. Slowly, he began following the little girl, hand over hand. He forced himself not to look down. He could feel sweat trickling down his face and running into his eyes. He blinked it away. The little girl reached the bear and stopped. Ricky was almost there.

Suddenly, she started to stand up. Ricky threw his left arm forward on the beam, then his right, and reached her just as she lost her balance. His left arm grabbed her around the waist. He felt the nausea coming up into his throat as his body lurched from side to side. He was sure he would lose his grip on the beam, but it held. He hung there by his right arm, his left arm holding the little body close to his chest. "Hang on," he whispered, to the child. Vaguely, he could hear cheering. His right arm began aching from the weight and the stretching. "Lord, help! I can't hold on much longer!"

Hang on, a voice seemed to reply.

Then, he heard a screech. Someone had figured out how to release the brakes on the scaffolding. Everyone was pushing it toward Ricky. Several men had jumped onto the scaffold before it started moving. Their arms reached out to grab Ricky and pull him up onto the scaffold. They had to pry his fingers off the beam. He didn't let go of the little girl until he was lying flat on his back on the scaffold looking up at his rescuers, many of them dressed in blue and wearing badges. He closed his eyes. "I give up," he said softly and lifted both hands to receive handcuffs.

He was helped to his feet and slapped on the back. They could see his knees were weak, and they held him up. They were calling him a hero. Ricky blinked from flashes of light from cameras. One man said he was a television reporter. The little girl was crying now, unhurt but frightened by all the commotion. "Don't cry," he said softly. "It's okay now."

She stopped crying and looked up at him and smiled. Her mother came rushing onto the scaffold and grabbed her, sobbing. A man was right behind her, and he tenderly helped them both off the scaffold. A moment later, he returned. He stood before Ricky, his face wet with tears. "Thank you!" He held out his hand. Ricky responded, and as they shook hands, the man suddenly grabbed him and hugged him. "Thank you," he said again. "Anything you want, you've got it! I can never repay you for saving Rosie."

Ricky smiled, "Rosie? My sister is Rosalita."

"Rosie is Rosalita. Her mother is from Mexico. Hey, if you don't have plans, have dinner with us. We would like to get to know you."

Ricky glanced at the guards and shook his head.

"I'm illegal," he said softly. "With all this, I might as well give up now. I'll be deported by tomorrow anyway."

"Oh, I don't think so. We can never have too many brave men in this country. And you are that. Son, I'll adopt you if I have to. I'll adopt your whole family! How's that?"

Ricky looked at him dubiously.

The man laughed. "Son, I have pots of money, but only one little girl. You saved my heart."

And with that, John Willings, sole owner of the largest pharmaceutical company in the world, put his arm around the slender boy's shoulders and walked him over to his wife and child and into America.

AFTER THE FIRE

I t had only been three days since the fire. Callie stared at what had been her mother's house. The fire had been devastating. If Jean next door hadn't seen the flames and called 911... Callie shuddered at the thought of what could have been. The fireman had carried her mother, Ellen, out of the burning house, still groggy from the sleeping pill she had taken. Then, Jean had called Callie. Callie threw a coat over her pajamas and came right away, but...

Before she got there, before her mother was even fully awake, the house was gone, burned to the ground. Callie's parents had moved into the house when they married. When her father died just after their forty-second anniversary, Callie wanted her mother to come live with her. Her husband liked Ellen, and they had extra space with the boys grown and gone and only Katy left at home. But Ellen said she couldn't leave her house. "I can't leave the memories," she had said. "I feel close to John here." Now, three years later, the fire had turned all the memories to ashes, and the wind was blowing them away.

Yesterday morning, Callie's mother had asked her to come back with her to see if anything had survived, anything at all. When they pulled in the driveway, Ellen looked bewildered. "Where is the house?" she whispered. Callie got out of the car and went around and opened her mother's door. Ellen stepped tentatively out of the car, one hand whitely clutching the edge of the door, the other covering her mouth.

She stared up at the oak tree that had always stood like a sentinel in front of the house. She and John had planted the tree the day they moved into the house. They had watched it grow through the years. It had towered over the house. But now, charred and gouged, it's foliage gone, it's bark burned away, it waited to be chopped down and removed.

Her gaze lowered to the yard. She stared first at the gouges in the grass from the firetruck tires and ladders, the hard sprays of water, and the fireman dragging equipment. Then she looked up. Where the house should be, she saw only blackened ashy ground, the broken cement blocks of the basement walls, rubble.

"Oh, John," she said softly. She started crying then, deep sobs, covering her face with both hands. Callie tried to pat her arm, but she turned away. She climbed back into the car and put her head down. "Take me away from here. Please take me away from here," she sobbed. Callie sadly closed the car door, and they drove back to Callie's house. The only sound in the car was her mother's sobs.

Her mother hadn't spoken since. At least, not while she was awake. But when she slept, she tossed and turned and mumbled about teacups from Aunt Rose and the painting John bought when they went to Boston one year and the old doll from her grandmother, and the oil painting of Callie when she was so very small. Memories that had lived in the cabinets and hung on the walls. All gone.

Today was Christmas Eve. Callie had come back to the house alone this morning hoping to find—what? A picture maybe, something, anything. She had been digging and sifting for hours. She found some bits of glass, a spoon, a twisted lump of metal she couldn't even identify. Callie held up her hand and watched the ashes and rubble drift down between her fingers. For the hundredth time, she shook her head. "This is hopeless," she whispered. "There's nothing left."

Her mind knew this was true, but her heart just couldn't accept it. "Oh, Mama, I'm so sorry. I wanted so much to find something for you, but everything is gone." She started to stand up, her hand shading her eyes from the bright sun. She closed her eyes to blink away the tears. When she opened them, she saw a sparkle in the rubble a few feet away. Another bit of broken glass, she thought, probably not worth picking up. Still, she went to check it. She bent down and carefully brushed some of the dirt away. The object was larger than she thought.

She kneeled down and uncovered more. It was a glass figure about four inches high. A lady in a long gown. It looked familiar. She pushed her hands down along the sides of the figure and started to pick it up. As the dust and debris fell off, she could see it was an angel with delicate lacy wings coming up and out from the figure's back. She stared at it.

"How could you have survived?" she wondered aloud. "You're not broken at all. But that's not possible.

You should be melted or broken into tiny bits."
Suddenly, she realized what she was holding. This was
the angel her mother tied to the top of the Christmas
tree every year. Everyone teased her because it was
so small, but she always said it didn't matter. Angels
and heroes could be any size, she said. What was in
the heart was what counted. Love in your heart made
you sparkle. And angels were filled with love, so they
sparkled a lot. The angel was kept in the china cabi-
net when it wasn't atop a Christmas tree. She turned
the figure over in her hand. Even dusty, it sparkled in
the sunlight. Callie smiled. When she was small, just
looking at the angel had made her feel brave.

Callie stood up. She stretched her cramped back
and sighed as she walked to the car. She laid the
angel carefully on the passenger seat, looked at it for
a moment, then started the car and drove home.

When she reached the house, she picked up the
angel and went inside. She stopped just inside the
entryway. She could hear her husband, Gary, talking
to her mother. Ellen was using the guest room just to
the left of the sunroom. She heard Gary quietly urging
Ellen to come out to the kitchen and have a cup of coffee, but Ellen refused. "I just want to sleep," she said.

Katy was standing in the doorway looking into
the guest room. She ran to Callie and hugged her.
"Grandma won't talk to me."

Callie kissed her. "Grandma is just very sad. Just
wait, Katy, okay?" Katy nodded.

"Mama?" Callie called. "Mama, I found something.
Look what I found."

She held out the angel to her mother. Even in the
house with only the lamplight, and still dusty, the

angel sparkled as if lit with an inner fire. Ellen sat up and peered at the angel for several moments. Then she reached out her hand, palm up, and accepted it from Callie. She looked down wonderingly at the angel.

"Where did you find her?" she asked in a shaky voice.

"In the rubble," Callie replied. "She was covered with debris and dust. I just saw a sparkle and started digging. Is she the treetop angel?"

"Yes," Ellen whispered. "But, how... Callie, she was on top of the tree when I went to bed. How?"

"Wow! She made it through the fire, Grandma. Just like you," said Katy.

"Tell us about her, Mama."

Ellen continued to stare at the tiny angel. How could she have survived that fire? She was not even chipped. She was perfect. But, then how had she survived all these years?

Ellen told them about the angel. She had belonged to John's grandmother in the old country, made for her by her husband as a wedding gift, a perfect hand-blown glass angel. She had traveled in a little box in Grandma's only trunk when the family came to the new country as immigrants. Every year, she was tied to the top of the Christmas tree. In the hard years, when the family had no Christmas tree, she was carefully hung from a ribbon tied to a nail in the wall. She was handed down through the years, and eventually became John's. She was always there.

Every year, Ellen would tie the angel to the top of the tree just like all the mothers before her had done. And every year, when the family gathered together, they would look up at the tiny angel and remember all the stories, and they would talk and laugh. And the children would listen wide-eyed as they stared wonderingly at the fragile bit of glass, an angel surprisingly strong like their family. Ellen loved the angel and all of the Christmas stories. Ellen told the stories, and Gary and Callie and Katy listened. And after a while, Ellen stopped talking and looked intently at the three of them.

"Callie, I want to give the angel to you."

"Oh no, Mama! She's the only memory I could find for you."

"No," Ellen said firmly as she opened Callie's hand and laid the angel in her palm. "No, Callie. She is just a figure that helped me remember some things. But she isn't the memory, the people are. I almost forgot that. Things don't matter really. You and Gary and Katy and all the rest of the family, you are my heart, you are my memories. When I look at you, I see John in your eyes and your smile. When I look at Katy, I see Gary and you and my mother and so many others. I am blessed with family. The angel just helped me remember that."

Ellen patted Callie's cheek. "That this tiny piece of glass has survived all these years is a miracle. Like the miracle of a family surviving. I'm going to be fine, Callie. I don't need the house or any of the things in it to remember John. I will remember him every time I look at you."

Callie hugged her mother and her husband and her daughter. Then, she laid the angel on the mantle next to the Christmas tree. She got some string from the kitchen drawer and the three-step ladder from the hall closet. She set up the ladder next to the tree and climbed up. Then she carefully tied the tiny, dusty, sparkly angel to the top of the tree.

"Grandma, tell me some more angel stories and all the fun stuff at Christmas."

Ellen looked at Katy and smiled.

"Okay," she said. "I remember when your mom was little.."

THE BAG LADY'S BOX

I hate being here, I thought angrily. After an hour of serving food to homeless people, I wanted out. I would never have volunteered for this, but the judge ordered it, so I had no choice. But, I didn't have to like it.

I scowled as I plopped mashed potatoes on the plate. I didn't look up as I held it out for the next "client" to take. These people, lines and lines of them. I tried not to look at them. Where do they come from? Where do they go when they leave here? Where do they sleep? I shook my head angrily. Forget them. Never get involved; that's my motto. I was never going to wind up like this. I hoped.

"Hey, lady, take the plate!" a gruff male voice snapped. "You're always looking in that stupid box!"

I looked up. Standing in front of me, a serene smile on her face, was a very old woman. At her neckline, I could see many different collars under a very worn and soiled coat. She was very small, and the coat covered her almost to the ground. The coat had two pockets, and I could see more pockets had been sewn on. Papers, a spoon, and a bit of a muffin stuck out of the tops of the puffed-out pockets.

She's a bag lady, I thought. *I bet everything she has is in those pockets.* She was holding a small, velvet-covered box, worn and soiled, the velvet scraped in places, a bedraggled, frayed ribbon barely attached to the cover. The cover was open, and she gazed dreamily down into the box. I stretched up, but I couldn't see what was in the box.

"Ma'am?" I called softly, then louder, "Ma'am." I held the plate out closer to her. She didn't seem to see it. The gruff man was next in line. He was impatient, and now he was getting angry. He lifted his hand as if to push or shove her. I reached over the counter and grabbed his hand to stop him. It surprised him, and he backed up. When I let go of his hand, the woman looked up. She closed the box, put it into her pocket, then took the plate from my outstretched hand. "Thank you," she said softly, her face almost glowing. She turned to the man. "I'm sorry to hold you up. Please forgive me." Her voice was lovely, well-modulated, and gracious.

"What's in that box, anyway?" he demanded. "My treasure," she replied simply.

"Treasure?" He exploded in laughter. "Yeah, right. You're so rich, you have treasure." His voice was mocking and cruel. "Get out of the way!" he snarled as she started to move away. She smiled, then turned and walked over to the first table and sat down. She seemed oblivious to his words.

"Gimme that!" he said, grabbing the plate from me. He started to follow the woman. Two men blocked his way. He tried to push his way through, then stopped when they wouldn't give way. He scowled at the men for a moment, then turned from them and went to a table on the other side of the room. He set the tray down, turned once to glare at the woman, then sat down with his back to her. She didn't seem to notice any of it.

I continued filling plates, watching her from the corner of my eye. She ate slowly, carefully cutting the food into small bites, looking around as she chewed. Occasionally, someone walked by her, and she would smile when they touched her arm and said, "Hi, good to see you. How are you doing?"

"Very well, thank you. And you?" was always her reply. More often than not, the person would sit down and start talking to her. She rarely spoke, just smiled and listened, really listened. Sometimes she would pat the person's arm or cheek. She really seemed to care about what they said.

People started leaving. The gruff man left. He glared at the woman just before he walked out the door. I was glad to see him go.

"She's really something, isn't she?" I turned to the young man standing behind me. "I can take over now," he said, "if you want to leave."

I started to say, "I can't wait to leave," but the words stuck. Instead, I said, "Who is she?"

He shook his head. "I don't know. A homeless lady. She won't tell anybody her name. She comes every day for dinner; that's all I know. She kinda brightens the place up, though, don't you think?" He smiled and glanced over at her. "Everybody likes her. She listens. That's the thing, she listens. I sat and talked to her once, talked a while. When I thought about it later, I realized I did all the talking, and she just listened. I was pretty down that day. She just listened and patted my hand. And then things just didn't seem so bad anymore. Funny, huh?"

"Where does she live? How does she live? It's so cold out." I paused. "Her coat doesn't look very warm."

He shook his head again. "I don't know. She never talks about herself. I asked a couple of the regulars, but they don't know either." He laughed, sounding embarrassed. "You know, I actually thought about following her once when she left, just to see where she went." He paused. "I never did, though.

"What's in the box, the little box she put in her pocket?"

"I don't know. I don't think anybody knows. I asked her once, and she just smiled. She said it was her treasure like it was full of diamonds or something. Weird, huh?"

He was taking off his apron. All the people had been served. Other volunteers would clear the tables and wash up everything. We were done. I took my apron off and hung it on the hook near the kitchen door.

I glanced over and saw her getting up, pulling her coat close around her neck. A little girl ran over and shyly held out a fuzzy scarf. The woman looked for the child's mother, who smiled and nodded. She nodded back. Then she accepted the scarf and bent down to hug the little girl who hurried back to her mother. The woman wrapped the scarf around her neck and slowly started for the door. Many people said goodbye to her and reached for her hand as she passed. Many of them handed her rolls and apples. She put them in her pockets. For later, I thought.

I'm not sure what got into me. I grabbed my jacket, my warm down-filled, fleece-lined jacket, and started after her. "Let me know where she goes," an amused voice said behind me. I kept going.

As I opened the door, snow blew in my face. Outside, the temperature had dropped. It must be well below freezing, I realized. I pulled on my cap and gloves. As warmly dressed as I was, I could still feel the bitter cold. I could see her up ahead walking slowly. She had pulled the scarf up so it covered her hair. I wondered if she had gloves.

I followed her. It wasn't hard. The wind was swirling the snow around, whipping it into my face and down my collar. Sometimes I couldn't see her at all for a moment, but I could see her footprints in the snow. I didn't see anyone else. We might have been the only two people in the world. I bent my head down against the onrushing stinging snow.

We weren't more than two blocks from the mission house when she screamed. She was under a streetlight. I saw someone knock her down. "Make a fool of me, will you?" a gruff voice shouted. He was hitting her with his fists. "I'll show you!"

I stared at the two of them. The man looked so big. I took a step back, and then he kicked at her, and I started running, the soft, wet snow sticking to my legs.

"What's in that box that's so great?" he snarled. "Your treasure? I bet it's some money. She lay on the ground moaning. "You can have it if you need it," she said softly. "It's okay. I'll give it to you."

"You bet you will!" He ripped off the little pocket and snatched the box. He held it up gleefully. He laughed as he yanked open the lid and dumped the contents into his hand. The laughing stopped as he stared for a moment, puzzled. Then he threw all of it at her. It fell around her into the snow. "It's junk!" he yelled angrily. "Junk! I thought it would be something I could sell, but it's just junk!"

He pulled a knife from his pocket. It gleamed as he held it up. "You're gonna regret fooling me." I watched as the knife came down towards her. That's when I tackled him. He was a lot bigger than me. I still can't believe I did that. I grabbed his arm. I could see she was bleeding. I hoped the cut wasn't deep. I tried to make him drop the knife by hitting his wrist against my leg. He was too strong. He knocked me down and was on me with the knife. He stabbed at my arms and face, connecting but not cutting deep. He aimed at my throat. *I'm going to die*, I thought. *I can't stop him.* I was hitting him with one fist and trying to hold the knife away with the other. The knife came closer and closer. I could hear him laughing in my ear.

Suddenly, he jerked his head away and fell to the side. The woman was hitting him with something, a rock. He was dodging and stabbing the knife at her. She screamed in pain. I jumped up and double-fisted the arm with the knife. The knife dropped to the ground. I turned to look at the woman. The man jumped back and started running.

She wasn't moving. I felt her pulse. It was there but not very strong. I shook her, but she didn't respond. There was no one around to help. I called 911 on my cell phone. All we could do was wait. I was afraid to move her, but it was so cold. I took off my gloves and put them on her icy hands. I rolled her slightly to get my coat around her. It looked like she had cuts and bruises all over her face and neck. The cold was probably stopping her from bleeding. I would have run back to get the car, but I was afraid that crazy man would come back. I could hear a siren in the distance now.

"My box," she moaned. "My treasure."

The ambulance came, and they took her to the hospital. My cuts weren't big enough to bother with, not like hers. They gave me my coat and gloves and told me to go home. I was suddenly freezing. I started to walk back to my car, but I went back. I found the box, but I didn't know what had been in it. I felt around the area where she had fallen, but what was I even looking for? I took off my gloves and felt the ground all around where she had fallen. All I could find were two little ornaments: a violin and a horn. They didn't look valuable, but it was all I could find. I threw them in the box and closed it. I was suddenly very tired, very confused. I tried to save her life, and she saved mine. That must mean something. Even for a punk like me.

I walked back to the soup kitchen. The lights were out. My car was still there. I climbed in and held the box up and looked at it all around. I didn't open it. I drove home. When I got there, I put the box on the table next to my bed, took a hot shower, drank some hot tea, looked through my mail, then stood in front of the large front window staring blankly out at the snow still falling, swirling in the wind. I finally fell asleep in a chair.

I awoke to the phone ringing. The police had found the man and needed me to ID him. I was happy to oblige. I grabbed some breakfast and turned on the TV. The woman's face was on the screen. She was still unconscious and had no identification. "If you know her, call…"

Finally, I got to the hospital.

The woman was going to be all right. She was awake and eating breakfast. Sunlight was streaming in the window. She was bruised, and her wrist was broken. The cuts were stitched and bandaged. The large one at her throat looked huge, but it was going to be all right. She saw my reflection in the window and turned and smiled when I came into the room. She told me her name was Louise. Her daughter had seen her on the TV and called the hospital. She wanted her to come live with her. She loved her.

I handed her the little box. "Ohhh, you found it," she whispered. She opened it and looked at the little ornaments. Then she looked up at me.

"I found them at the park," I said, "but I didn't know if they were from your box."

She nodded. "Yes, they are. My daughter plays the violin. I used to play the horn. We played together just for the joy of it. It was so wonderful. That is what I heard every time I opened the little box. The wonderful music, the memories."

She looked down into the box, her eyes closed, her head swaying as she remembered.

"Now you'll be able to hear her really play again," I said.

She didn't answer. I repeated it. Still, she didn't respond. The nurse came in with a little cup with a pill in it. "Time for meds," she called.

Louise didn't look up. The nurse came to the bed and gently touched Louise's arm. Louise looked up. "Time for meds," she said. Louise smiled.

She saw the surprise in my face. "I have been deaf for a long time. When it happened, and I realized I would never hear again, I would never play again, I was so angry. I had to learn to read lips, but it was so hard. I resented everyone who could hear. I was mean and angry. I drove everyone away, even my daughter. I became a horrible person. I lost my job, then my house, then everything else. Except this little box, the last gift from my daughter."

She was quiet for a long time, then she said, "I had nothing, and I figured that's what I deserved. I just didn't care about anything anymore—until tonight. You risked your life to save me. I must have some value for you to do that. I'm going to try again. Thank you." She patted my arm, and I finally understood.

We talked more. I left when her daughter came. I stood outside the hospital for a long time, thinking. She risked her life to save me, and I risked my life to save her. *Maybe we both have value*, I thought. I smiled. That's what my mom always said to me, "You have value."

When I was in prison, I never answered her letters; I was too ashamed. When I got out, I thought about calling her, but... I took her last letter out of my pocket. It was wrinkled and faded now. I was never without it. Like the little box Louise hung onto. I read the letter. "Come home," she wrote. That was what she had said in every letter, come home. Maybe it was time now.

I thought of the mission house and the people there, people like Louise, like me. If I hurried, I could help serve lunch. And then, maybe I could make a phone call and start a real life. I turned my face up and smiled as the new snow softly landed on my face, clean and crisp. Just like me.

FINDERS KEEPERS

"**M**anagement has agreed that if you return the money and sign a confidential confession, we won't call the police. Pressing charges would just bring bad publicity. Obviously, you can no longer work here."

Karen was stunned. "What money? What are you talking about?"

Barbara shook her head. "You were seen taking it yesterday. A witness came forward and signed an affidavit. We found the money wrappers in your office just like he said." Barbara stood up. "Oh, Karen, how could you? I always thought you were one of the most honest people I ever met. Now..."

A guard accompanied her to her desk and stood there while she packed up her few personal things in a brown paper bag then he escorted her out of the building. Everyone stared as they passed. When the front door closed behind her, the tears came. It was the day before Christmas.

She remembered last night when she got home from work. Tommy was jumping up and down with excitement. "Six weeks!" he screamed. "You did it! You did it! The probation is done. Starting tomorrow, you're a real employee! Mom, you did it!"

It was cold, the snow falling lightly, softly. Her head was bare, and gusts of wind were blowing her short, curly hair. She started shivering. It wasn't fair. They fired her. For stealing! She would never steal. Never! She was an honest person. She took pride in being known as an honest person. What would Tommy think? My mom is a thief?

It had been so hard since Jack died. She and Tommy reassured each other they would make it through. And they did. But they got behind on things, like the rent and utilities. Their landlord was nice about it, but he made it clear if they didn't catch up by the first of the year, they would have to move. "It's not fair," she sobbed. "I've been trying so hard. It's just not fair."

She took a deep breath and headed toward the parking lot. The snow was turning to sleet, stinging her face. Her hair was turning into a frozen hat as the snow filled in all the curls. She was between a van and her car when she tripped on something and fell sideways, hitting her head on the van's tire. She dropped the bag, and photos slid out into the snow. She laid there, her back jammed against the tire, her legs wedged under the van. She could see a large can covered with Christmas designs next to her car door. That must be what she tripped over. As she struggled to get up, she felt an arm pulling her upright. She looked up and smiled at the very short oriental-looking woman helping her up.

"Thank you!" Karen said. The woman spoke but not in English. She sounded upset, angry. Karen asked,

"Do you speak English?" The woman shook her head. The woman pointed at Karen's car, then at Karen. Karen nodded and unlocked her car door and got in. The woman picked up the photos and put them into the bag then handed it and the can to Karen. Karen took them in a daze. The woman started crying, said something Karen didn't understand then climbed into the van and drove away.

Karen drove home, left the bag and the can on the kitchen table, and climbed into bed. She fell asleep and didn't wake until she heard Tommy calling from the kitchen, "Mom, I'm home."

How could she tell him? What would he say?

She came slowly out to the kitchen. Tommy was sitting at the table carefully counting stacks of money. Many stacks. Many, many stacks!

"Hi, Mom," he said brightly. "Did you rob a bank?"

Karen's mouth fell open. "Where did that money come from?"

"The can. I counted fourteen thousand and eighty-five dollars so far. There's a lot more."

"Oh, Tommy. Someone stole money at work and blamed me. I got fired. I fell over this can in the parking lot. The lady that helped me up threw it in my car. I didn't know there was money in it." She paused. "Tommy, I don't have a job anymore!"

They sat at the table for a while looking at the stacks of money.

"We've got to take this money to the police," Karen said softly. "Put the money back in the can, Tommy. The police will hold it until they find the owner."

"What if they never find the owner?"

Karen thought a moment. "I think we get to keep it if no one claims it. But I think they look for a long time."

Tommy shook his head. "Mom, you know," he said softly, "if we kept just a little of this money, we could catch up on the rent and then we wouldn't have to be homeless next week."

"Homeless? Who told you that?"

"The landlord." He paused. "Mom, are you sure we should give the money to the police?"

She sighed and nodded. "Yeah, and I think we should do it right away before we get too tempted." She looked at the can. There was a silver monogram letter on the front. It might help find the owner. Who puts money in a Christmas tin?

She looked out the window. It got dark early, and it was snowing. She really didn't want to go out, but... She looked back at Tommy and at the can. It was so much money, and it was so tempting. What would it be like in a homeless shelter?

"Tommy, I'm going to call the police right now and ask them to send an officer to get this money. I don't want to keep it here."

"I wonder whose money it is?" Tommy said aloud.

Karen shook her head. She was already dialing. She spoke briefly on the phone then hung up.

"An officer will stop by this evening. We'd better get dinner; it's getting late."

Karen turned on the small TV on the kitchen counter. The news was just starting. She listened while she scrambled eggs and Tommy made toast. Traffic was very slow, and there was a pileup on the freeway because of the snow. Then a small woman with almond-shaped eyes was holding a picture of a little boy of about three, and talking through an interpreter, pleading for kidnappers to return her son. "I gave her the money," she said, "but she did not bring my boy back. Please, please." The woman began sobbing. Karen glanced up and gasped. "That's the woman from the parking lot. She must have thought I was the kidnapper. That's why she threw the can in my car. She was paying the ransom!" Tommy's mouth fell open. He stared at the TV.

"Mom, the kidnappers didn't get the money, we have it. What about the little boy?"

The doorbell rang.

"The police, Mom! We can tell them what happened. They can find the little boy. Right?" Tommy's face was pale.

"Sure, Tommy. They'll find him."

Karen went to the door and looked through the peephole. She frowned. She could see two men outside the door. They didn't look like policemen. They were roughly dressed, and one carried a pole of some kind and kept hitting it against his palm. They looked mean. The kidnappers? They must have been watching at the parking lot.

The doorbell rang again. Karen knew that because the peephole was hidden on the edge of the doorframe, the men wouldn't know she could see them. She looked again. Now only one man was there. She tried to see further, but the sight was limited. The man was looking to the side and talking. She couldn't hear him. When he looked back at the door, he was smiling. It was not a nice smile. She backed away from the door. She turned to Tommy with her finger on her lips. He looked confused. Karen came close and whispered, "Men in the hall, one left, they're not police, I think they're the kidnappers." Tommy's eyes got big.

Karen turned off the lights and the TV and peeked out the window. They were on the third floor, but there was a fire escape outside the kitchen window. They could go down that. Wait. There was a man in the alley. She watched in horror as the man jumped up trying to reach the fire escape. Then he walked away. Her relief was short lived when a moment later she heard a car coming down the alley. The car stopped just below the fire escape. The engine stopped, and the driver got out. It was the same man. He was trying to climb on top the car. If he reached the fire escape, he could be in the apartment in just a few minutes. She grabbed the phone to call 911. There was no dial tone.

Tommy was staring down at the man. Karen grabbed Tommy's arm and pulled him down the hall and into the bathroom. She dumped the dirty clothes hamper and had Tommy climb in.

"Be very quiet," she said, "Don't come out or make a sound until I come back for you."

Tommy nodded. She kissed his forehead and smiled, then threw the dirty clothes on top of him and closed the cover. It had ventilation holes in the sides, so she knew he would get enough air even though it wouldn't be comfortable. She closed the bathroom door and hurried back to the kitchen.

She peeked out the window. The man still hadn't gotten on top of the car. She grabbed the can and unlocked the window, then eased it open. She knew if he saw her, he would follow her, especially if he saw the can. Tommy would be safe.

She prayed for all the help she could get, then climbed out the window and started up the fire escape. She knew the roof door was kept locked, but her plan was to break a window and climb into one of the apartments and then go out their front door screaming. If she could rouse the tenants, maybe the men would leave. But, wait. If the men left, the little boy might never come home. She stopped. Think, think. Two doors over from her apartment there was a vacancy. If she could break that window and get in....

She went back down to the third floor. She was moving quietly, but the man below saw her and yelled. She moved faster to the windows of the vacant apartment. She smashed the can against the window, but it didn't break. She hit it several more times. It still didn't break. Now what? She glanced around. A broken grill was leaning against the wall just a few feet from the window. She grabbed it and threw it at the window. It bounced off, but she heard the window crack. She caught it before it fell off the side and threw it again. This time, the window broke more. She threw herself at the cracked window, and it shattered around her. She fell into the kitchen.

She had many small cuts, but she didn't even notice them. She looked around for something to drop on the car and throw at the man. The apartment was empty. Of course, it was empty; no one lived here. She looked at the gas stove. Then she opened the can and took out some bills. She turned on a burner and lit a bill and ran to the bedroom and held it up to the fire alarm. She lit three bills before the alarm went off. She knew it would trigger a call to the fire station. They were close by and would be here in minutes.

She unplugged the microwave and ran with it to the window. The man was just coming in. She threw it at him, and he fell down. With all her strength, she picked it up again and smashed it down on his head. She really hoped he wasn't dead, but she didn't have time to check. He was down and not moving. That was enough.

She climbed out the window and looked out over the edge of the fire escape. No one else was there. She picked up the battered microwave and threw it down at the car. It crashed onto the hood. It didn't look like it did much damage. She heard a noise behind her and turned just as the other man grabbed for her. He had come out of her apartment. She could only pray Tommy was still safe. The tenants were coming out the windows and down the fire escape. The man must have realized he would be caught. He went down the fire escape and ran to the car.

Just then, the fire engine turned into the alley, its horn blaring. The car was facing the engine. The man turned and started running down the alley. A police car pulled into the other end of the alley. The man stopped, turned to look back at Karen just getting off the fire escape, then sat down on the ground and put his hands behind his head. Karen started to turn to go back up the fire escape when she glanced at the car. She was behind the car, and in the back window was a little boy pounding on the glass and screaming.

She ran to the car and tried to open the back door. It was locked. The front door wasn't. She opened the door and reached her arms out to the little boy. "It's all right," she said softly. "Come, come to me. It's all right." The boy stared at her, obviously terrified then suddenly threw himself over the seat into her arms. She held him tight as a policeman helped her out of the car. Firemen and policemen were everywhere. She looked up toward her apartment and saw Tommy waving at her from the fire escape. She waved back, then held the boy tightly as she told the policeman everything that had happened.

He sent other policemen to get the second man and the can. The policeman helped her back up to her apartment and the boy's mother was called. The boy clung to Karen but accepted a cookie from Tommy. When his mother arrived, he jumped from Karen's lap and ran to mom. The little boy cried, his mom cried, Karen cried, Tommy cried, and even the policeman got tears in his eyes.

There were actually three kidnappers. The policeman who had been sent to pick up the can of money caught the third one breaking in Karen's apartment door. He recognized him as the man the mother had identified as one of the kidnappers and called for reinforcements. The squad car arrived just in time to stop the guy in the alley. The reporters showed up and took many pictures. One reporter talked a lot with Tommy. The landlord happily boarded over the broken window and blew kisses to Karen.

The next day, Christmas Day, Karen's picture was on the front page next to a smaller picture of her son grinning, with the caption, "My mom is my hero."

It was a great story. "Heart-warming," the editor called it. "An honest woman, a brave mother, rescuing a little boy. Heart-warming."

The ransom had been $25,000. The boy's family tried to give Karen all the money, but she refused, so they quietly talked to her landlord and paid her rent for a year. That was nice.

The newspaper had some openings and offered her a job. She accepted. They figured there was always room for an honest person, especially a brave, honest person. The handsome policeman asked her for a date. She accepted.

Matthews and Brown, her former employer, after investigating further, determined that the "witness" was the one who actually stole the money. They called to apologize and give her a bonus and her job back. She took the bonus but declined the job.

Karen and Tommy sat together on the couch reading the paper. Every once in a while, they would look up and smile at each other. It was Christmas, they had each other, and sure enough, things were getting better.

"Boy, Mom, if you hadn't called the police to come get the money, those guys might have taken the money and got away. They might have killed us. And the little boy. I didn't know you were so brave. And it all worked out because you're honest. I'm proud of you, Mom."

"I'm glad you're proud of me, Tommy. I'm proud of both of us. I think our guardian angels must have been working overtime. But Tommy, being honest by turning in the money wasn't a big deal. Anyone would do the same."

"Mom, if it wasn't a big deal, we wouldn't be on the front page!"

THE DOVE

The woman had run as far as she could, she could not run any more. She ran with her arms crossed, clutching a bag to her chest. Her legs trembled with exhaustion, and her chest hurt from the running. She climbed the steps to the doorway of the partially destroyed building and slipped inside. The door was hanging by one hinge, swinging in the wind. It was cold in the building. She climbed and stumbled over the rubble as she hurried up the stairs to the second floor, slipping on the ice and snow that lay in piles throughout the bombed-out structure. She saw another stairway, and fear pushed her to continue to the third floor. She stopped there.

There were no more stairs. Most of the roof was gone. The back wall had fallen away. She searched for a place to hide. She saw a door and went through it, closing the door behind her. There was rubble everywhere, much of it from the roof and a hole in the far wall, but the outside corner of the room was still intact. The brickwork of a damaged fireplace had kept the corner from collapsing. It was there that the woman sank exhausted to the floor. She backed into the corner until her back was to the wall. For a moment, she sat very still, listening. No one had followed her into the building. She was safe. For a few minutes, anyway, she was safe.

Carefully she opened the thin cloth bag. The baby was still sleeping. She smiled at the infant and kissed his cheek. She opened the front of her threadbare coat and closed up the child inside. Even in the shelter of this corner, she felt the sting of the sleet falling through holes in the roof and blowing across the open floor.

The child woke but did not cry, ignoring the sleet, the sound of bombs falling, people screaming, oblivious to everything except his mother's warmth and milk and the safety of her arms.

The young mother leaned back and closed her eyes as the baby nursed. Suddenly her eyes widened with fear at the sound of heavy boots running up the stairs. In her world, there were only soldiers and victims. She was not a soldier.

Outside, there were shouts. Soldiers were ordering people to line up. Some of the people had weapons and shouted back at the soldiers. The air was thick with fear and hatred—and war.

Some of the people prayed, "Please, Lord, bring peace." But there was no peace. The weapons were raised and pointed on both sides.

She looked around frantically for a hiding place. There was none.

The door was flung open.

A young soldier stood in the doorway. He glanced around the room, his weapon raised. Then he stared at the woman and the baby. He lowered the weapon a little.

"Take no prisoners. Those are my orders," he reminded himself aloud.

He was very young, this soldier, not much older than the mother cowering in the corner. *She is so young*, he thought. He glanced at the baby in her arms, only the top of the baby's head showing above the opening of the woman's coat.

How old is that baby? he wondered. They said we must fight for our country, to protect our families. They said the enemy would kill us, kill our families, our babies. He shook his head. Take no prisoners. But surely they didn't mean young girls and babies. Surely...

But they did mean that.

Kill all the enemy, they said. Do not try to decide who should live and who should die. Kill them all. Take no prisoners.

He lifted his weapon and sighted it. The woman stood up slowly, shaking, her face pale. This would be the end of her life and her child's.

"Peace," she said softly pleading. She held out one hand, palm up. "That's all I want. Please."

The soldier blinked away the tears forming in the corners of his eyes. "I don't want to do this," he whispered.

Take no prisoners. Kill the enemy. She is the enemy. His hand moved to the trigger, and he froze. He stared at the baby.

"I can't do this."

They stood staring at each other, the young woman shielding her baby with her arms and the soldier, frozen with his finger on the trigger.

That's when the dove appeared. It was impossible, of course. It was snowing. A dove could not be here now, not now. Yet it was.

The dove hovered in the emptiness of the broken window. It looked first at the soldier as he lowered his weapon, then turned to the woman. She clutched the baby tighter and moved as if pulled toward the window.

The woman stood near the dove in the window opening. If she had looked down, she would have seen all of the weapons lowered, all of the people on both sides of this war looking up at the third-floor window. She saw none of it. She looked only at the dove.

The baby woke. He smiled and reached for the dove. The people below saw it. They saw the dove brush the infant's cheek and leave a feather in his hand. They heard the baby laugh.

The dove, still hovering in the window, turned toward the people outside.

Everyone stared at the dove. No one was surprised when it disappeared. The weapons stayed down. The people smiled at one another. Enemy looked at enemy and saw a person. And there was peace.

The war did not end, but there was peace. For a short while, there was peace in their hearts.

Men—and women and babies—can and must do what is right. And when they do, the impossible can happen. There are still miracles.

God still cares. And wherever men and women remember this, there can be peace.

THE OLD WOMAN

*K*en sprawled unconscious on the ground under the bridge. Slowly, his eyes opened, and he shook his head to clear the fog in his mind. Dimly, he could hear a voice, but no one was there. Where was he? His stomach rumbled with hunger, but he didn't notice. How long had he been asleep? He tried to stand and fell back down. The biting cold was stinging the exposed flesh: face, fingers, feet. But he didn't feel the cold. He did feel pain. His face hurt. His chest hurt when he breathed. Pain covered him like a blanket. What had happened? He closed his eyes and tried to remember. Slowly, his thoughts cleared.

He remembered the bar. People from work were there. Celebrating. Merry Christmas. He drank too much, as usual. He was supposed to meet Patsy and the boys for dinner at his mother's. One last drink, he had said to himself. Followed by another "one last drink." And another. When he finally said he was leaving, Jack and Rob had offered to drive him home or call a taxi, but he refused. They had even argued with him, but he'd started for the door, laughing and staggering.

They helped him to his car. They tried again to talk him out of driving, but he wouldn't listen. He never listened to anyone.

Of course, it was too late to meet Patsy. He had turned off his cell phone when he realized he was late for the dinner. He knew she would call and she would be angry or hurt or both. When he left for work that morning, she had tried to talk to him, reminding him of when they were first married, how happy they had been. Their lives had revolved around their family, their church. It was a good life. But now, he wasn't there for them anymore. He was out most every evening, and she knew he was drinking a lot. And when he was home, he yelled at the boys and her. It seemed like he was angry all the time. He said she was always nagging. He had to work, didn't he? He had to socialize with customers, have a few drinks. Nothing wrong with having a few drinks. She looked away, hurt and tired. She told him quietly that if he didn't make it to the dinner, they were through. She couldn't go on like this. He didn't believe her. She had said that before, and she didn't leave. After all, he wasn't purposely trying to hurt her. It was just… It was just… what?

He remembered getting into his car. Jack and Rob shook their heads, told him to be careful and went back to the bar. He started the engine and put the car into drive. He couldn't see very well. Everything was doubled and fuzzy, so he drove very slowly. There was no centerline because it was a side street. The curbs kept moving, so he tried to drive exactly between them. He concentrated hard, watching the curbs and snapping his eyes open when they started to close. Suddenly, the car hit something, and his body flew forward into the steering wheel and windshield, then backward, his head slamming into the headrest. The movement pulled his foot off the gas pedal, and it came down between the gas pedal and the brake. The engine was roaring loudly and unevenly. Someone pulled in front of me, he thought angrily. He fumbled with the door and finally got it open. He held on to the top of the car door as he pushed it open and got out.

The front of his car had pushed in the side of an old sedan. It was so rusty he couldn't tell what color it was. Five or six young people were standing around looking at the damage. One of them, a young girl, approached him.

"Are you okay?" she asked in a soft voice.

"No!" Ken shouted. "I'm not okay! You pulled right in front of me!" He pointed a shaky finger at the girl. "You are going to jail!"

The girl stepped back in surprise.

"But our car is parked at the curb. We weren't driving. Look, you ran into it sideways. It isn't even turned on. We were inside that house and heard the crash and came out to see what happened. You hit a parked car," she repeated.

The girl pointed her finger at him, and Ken exploded. His mind was hot with drunken rage. He couldn't really understand what the girl was saying, except she was trying to blame him! He threw himself at her, fists flying. She was caught by surprise and didn't even have time to get her arms up to protect herself. Ken's fist caught the girls chin and knocked her over. Ken laughed and kicked at the girl's stomach. He didn't connect and fell back against his car. As he slowly slid down the side of the car, he looked up to see several young men staring down at him. He couldn't understand what they were saying. As they came closer, he saw the anger in their faces. And he knew they were going to beat him to death.

In a sudden moment of clarity, he saw himself as they saw him. Shame filled his heart. He glanced at the girl being helped up by an older woman. She's pregnant, he realized and was appalled. He had kicked her. Did he hurt her? Did he hurt the baby? He closed his eyes and tears ran down his cheeks. He felt a blow to his chin, then his shoulder, then more blows. *I deserve it*, he thought. *I wish I were dead. Everyone would be better off.*

He stiffened his body against the next blow, not knowing where he would be hit. The blow never came. He heard a woman's voice. He opened his eyes. The old woman was holding her hands up palms open in front of the boys and talking rapidly. They were listening to her. One by one, the boys stepped back. She hugged them and patted their backs and spoke in a soft, gentle voice. She smiled at them, and they nodded and went back into the house. The young girl was the last to leave. She glanced back at Ken with pity.

She pitied him. His stomach lurched at the thought. He was pitied! He looked down at the ground and started to pity himself.

So, this is what I have become? he thought. *A drunken man who hits little girls and kicks pregnant women and yells at people I've hurt?*

"Yes," a strong, feminine voice answered him. "Yes, this is what you have become."

He looked up. The old woman was standing in front of him. But she did not pity him. She looked not angry but disappointed. Why should she be disappointed? She didn't even know him.

"Ah, but I do know you." Her voice penetrated the fog still swirling in his mind.

"Who are you? I don't know you." But even as he said this, he realized she looked familiar.

"You did know me. Before you grew up and embraced the world. Look closely at me. Listen to my voice. Do you remember, precious child?"

Precious child? No one had ever called him that except his grandmother. She said he was a precious child of God. But she died years ago.

"Yes, she did." The woman seemed to know his thoughts. "She gave you all the love in the world. And she told you stories of a love even greater than hers. Someone else who loves you even more than she did."

Suddenly he heard a siren. It sounded like it was coming this way. Those kids must have called the police! He forced himself to stand holding onto the still open car door. "I've got to get out of here," he said aloud. "If I get another DUI, they'll take my license. I could lose my job."

"Where will you go?" the old woman asked.

He glanced around at the darkness and felt real fear. Where could he go? He couldn't walk home. He didn't even know where he was—and he was too ashamed to call anyone.

He took a careful step forward. He was wobbly, and every step hurt. He couldn't think anymore. Run, he had to run. It didn't matter where, he just had to get away from here. He ran. Stumbling, falling, getting up again. As fast as he could, he ran. He ran until exhaustion and cold, and alcohol dropped him unconscious to the ground under the bridge.

Slowly his eyes opened. So here I am, *he thought. He peered up at the bridge but didn't recognize it. His body was shivering from the cold. He hurt all over, but he no longer felt the pain. He tried to stand up, but he couldn't move. He felt disconnected from his body.* I've got to get up, *he thought.* I'll freeze here. I'll die here. But I can't move. *Help. He mouthed the word, but no sound came out. He shook his head. The pain made him dizzy. Help. He saw the old woman watching him. Help, he called soundlessly to her as he slipped back into unconsciousness.*

The old woman sat a few feet from him, watching him. She did not intervene when a skinny young man in dirty, ragged clothes came by. He was repeatedly jerking his head to the side and talking out loud, "I'm so cold; my feet are so cold." He stopped when he saw Ken. He came slowly closer and pushed at Ken's foot and hand. When Ken didn't respond, he pulled off Ken's shoes and socks. He held them up in the dim light and examined them, then he nodded and took off his own shoes (they had holes in the bottom) and laid them carefully next to Ken's feet. He had no socks. He put on Ken's socks and shoes and closed his eyes and smiled at the sudden warmth around his feet. He probably would have taken Ken's coat too, but he heard a noise and ran.

Nor did the old woman stop a young man with an angry face who furtively stood over Ken with a knife, then kneeled down and removed his wallet. The young man smiled when he saw the cash, Ken's bonus, so much money. He put the money in his pocket and examined the credit cards and driver's license. He could get a good amount for them, the wallet too, real leather, not even worn. He thought about it for a moment then reached down with his other hand and pulled Ken's watch from his wrist. In the dim light, the young man looked over the watch. There was no inscription in back. He didn't take watches or jewelry with inscriptions, too easy to trace. He put the watch in his pocket. Did Ken have a tie clasp or ring? That was always good. No. He thought about taking Ken's coat. It looked expensive. And warm. *He'll probably freeze anyway*, he thought.

The old woman watched him. *But I already got a lot of money from the guy*, he thought. *And it is Christmas Eve.*

He tucked the wallet back in Ken's pocket. He was surprised by his own feelings. "Hey, man," he said softly, glancing around to be sure no one would hear him. "I hope you make it." He pulled the coat closer around the unmoving man. He felt something in the coat pocket. He pulled it out, a cell phone, a really nice one. He knew a guy that bought these fancy phones. Paid a fair price, too. He said he wiped them, and then they were untraceable. It would be nice to know how to do that. The phone was turned off. The boy stuck it into his pocket and then remembered something else the guy said. A lot of these cells, mainly the newer ones, had GPS in them. He remembered a television show where the police traced the phone and caught the guy who had it. He couldn't remember if the phone had to be on or not. *If I have his phone and the police trace it, they'll follow it right to me*, he thought. Too iffy, he decided. Nice phone, though. He didn't see the old woman watching him. He held the phone for a moment then smiled. "You know," he said aloud, looking down at Ken, "I got a pretty nice Christmas present from you, all that money. Maybe I'll give you one."

He flipped open the phone and turned it on. He dialed 911 and listened. He could hear the operator asking, "Where are you? What is the problem?" When no one answered her, he heard her asking someone there to try to trace the call. He smiled again and laid the phone on Ken's chest and stepped back. "Merry Christmas, man," he whispered, then he turned and ran under the bridge and up the other side. He was tempted to stick around and see how long it took the police to come, but that would be stupid. He ran down the street planning the gifts he would buy for his family and friends and himself. Part of him felt really good that he hadn't taken Ken's coat or wallet and especially that he had called 911. His mom didn't like what he did, but he thought he might tell her about this. She would be proud of him.

The old woman was still sitting there when the police car pulled up. They immediately called for an ambulance and called Ken's family on the cell phone. Home was programmed in. His wife was angry until she realized it was the police. She rushed to the hospital.

In the ambulance, they took his vitals and gave him oxygen and wrapped him in special heat blankets. He was sort of awake, but mostly not. The old woman sat beside him. Each time he opened his eyes, she was there gazing down at him. "Thanks," he said.

She shook her head. "It wasn't me," she said smiling. "It was someone much greater than me." She smiled just like his grandmother, but he knew she wasn't his grandmother. She talked like his grandmother too. "Look higher," she said. He looked up, and the light blinded him.

"Am I dying?" He closed his eyes, terrified. "I've got to tell Patsy how sorry I am first."

"You'll be fine," she said. "You have been given time. Be the man you were meant to be. Look."

Tentatively he opened his eyes. He saw images surrounded by a beautiful light. He saw a little boy, himself, who loved and believed. Then a young man, caring and kind, meeting his sweetheart at church and marrying her, making promises he meant to keep. Then the light darkened. He saw himself as he was now, ignoring his family, drinking himself into oblivion almost every night, cold, uncaring, afraid, wasting his time on people and things that didn't matter, didn't nourish him, ignoring that part of his life meant to nurture him and keep him whole. Love poured into his life, but he didn't accept it, and he didn't return it.

He started to sob. The EMTs talked to him and did what they could, but the pain, the real pain was in his heart, and they couldn't help him. He looked up at the old woman.

"Please help me," he begged.

"Do not ask me," she responded. "Ask the One who gives life and forgives all. He can bring you peace. Ask Him."

And he did ask. He begged and was told God's love was there for the asking. He asked for forgiveness and felt it unwinding and banishing the fears, the worries, the regrets. He knew he was forgiven. He asked for peace, and it was poured over him. By the time the ambulance reached the hospital, he was a changed man. And he wanted to stay that way. Without him even asking, God told him alcohol was no longer a part of his life; he did not need it any longer. And he breathed a sigh of relief.

In the emergency room, Ken looked for the old woman but didn't see her. He said to himself that he wanted to thank her, but really, he knew he just wanted to see her again. He had the nurse ask the police about the old woman. They never saw her. Neither did the ambulance crew. He thought about that.

His wife forgave him. She told him she had been praying for him. And their two boys had been praying for him, too. When she reached for his hand, he hugged her and sobbed, telling her over and over how sorry he was and how much he loved her and how different things were going to be.

He had a concussion, a cracked rib and many bruises caused by the accident, and he had twisted his ankle when he fell by the bridge. There were other bruises too. He never told the doctor or anyone about the boys beating him. *That beating saved my life*, he thought. The medication dulled the pain to a hard ache. *I'm alive*, he thought. *The bruises don't matter.* The doctors were surprised he didn't have frostbite and hypothermia. "God protected me," he told them. His wife overheard him and wondered.

The police told him his car was found. The young people had called the police after the accident and asked them to look for him because he was lost. *How right they were*, he thought. He admitted to the police the accident was his fault; he had been drinking. He knew he would probably lose his license, but he would live with the consequences.

Ken asked for the address where the accident occurred, and when he got out of the hospital, he went there and asked the young girl's forgiveness. It surprised her. She was gracious and forgave him. The boys, too, were genuinely concerned for him. They told him they had all prayed for him. The boys apologized for the beating. They were ashamed and swore they would never do anything like that again. Would the boys be arrested? He told them he had not told the police and he would not. He forgave them and hugged each one of the boys. Then he asked them about the old woman. They couldn't remember seeing an old woman. They said he must have imagined it.

It was three days before he told Patsy about the old woman. They were sitting in the living room together looking at the Christmas tree and the deep snow in the yard beyond the window.

"Patsy, do you believe me?" he asked.

Patsy smiled then and nodded her head. She hadn't seen the old woman, but she knew right away who had sent her. And now Ken knew, too.

TED AND THE PRINCESS

Most stories about princesses are fairytales, and they start with "Once upon a time." But not all of them. As you read some of them, you think this must have really happened. And when you finish the story and close the book—you wonder. Did it really happen? Or not? And then you think, does it matter?

Mrs. Baxter was very surprised when the doctor told her she was going to have a baby. She thought she was done having babies. She already had eight sons: the oldest was seventeen, the youngest eight. But when she got over being surprised, she was delighted.

She told her husband that evening. He was surprised, too. And then delighted.

They gathered the boys and told them. They were surprised. But they were not delighted.

"Another kid?" grumbled Andy, the oldest.

Then the others chimed in.

"Just what we need, another guy!"

"There isn't enough room at the table!"

"I'll never get into the bathroom now!"

"Do I still get to play hockey?"

"Where is he going to sleep?"

"He can't sleep in my room!"

"Eeww! Dirty diapers!"

"I'm not babysitting!"

Mom and Dad were dismayed by the comments, but they reasoned that since the boys loved each other and hung around together a lot, surely another little boy would be welcome when the time came.

The days passed quickly through the heat of summer and the beginning chill of fall. Then, on Christmas Eve, the whole family drove through a snowstorm to the hospital, and the baby was born.

They had talked a lot about a name. The boy's names were alphabetical.

Andy (Andrew),
   Chris (Christian),
      Bri (Brian),
         Davy (David),
Ed (Edward),
   Freddy (Frederick),
      Gerby (George),
         Happy (Harold).

The next letter was "I". No one could think of a name that started with "I" except Icarus. It was a weird name and his nickname would be "Icky." They all thought it would be a hilarious nickname, but Dad frowned and said not for his son.

While they sat in the waiting room debating names, Dad was in the delivery room with Mom. When he came out, he had a really silly grin. He just stood there grinning at them for a long time, then he laughed and said, "Boys, we need to start the name search over. It's a girl!"

"A girl?"

"What are we going to do with a girl?"

"We don't know anything about girls!"

"That means pink everything, doesn't it?"

"Where is she going to sleep?"

"She can't sleep in my room!"

"Poor mom!"

"I'm not babysitting a girl!"

"What are we going to name her?"

Dad said softly, "Come and see her, then we'll talk about names."

The boys stood up. They tried to be nonchalant but they were all eager to see the new baby, their sister. A sister! What could they do with a sister? They played rough all the time. Girls can't play rough. They stood in the doorway, a little afraid to enter the room. They peered around at each other until Mom said, "Come in, boys. Come and meet your new baby sister."

Slowly, they came forward in a line, oldest to youngest, to see the baby. Each peered down at her asleep on Mom's chest. Slowly, Mom unwrapped the receiving blanket so the boys could see her. She had only a tiny diaper on.

"She's so tiny."

"Her hair is red like yours, Mom."

"She's wrinkly."

"Her skin is kind of red."

"Her fingers are really long!"

"What color are her eyes?"

"I might let her sleep in my room."

"I might babysit her if she doesn't poop. Eww!"

After they looked at her, the boys crowded around the other side of the bed. Dad stood at the head of the bed smiling down at Mom.

"Surprised?" Mom asked.

The boys nodded. So did Dad. Mom grinned and nodded too.

"Guess we need to make some changes at home to accommodate a little girl," Mom said. Everyone nodded.

"Will you all help?" Dad asked. Again, everyone nodded.

"Well, then," Mom said, wrapping the baby again in the little blanket. "It's time you held your new sister."

The boys backed away from the bed, their eyes huge. None of them wanted to hold her. What if they dropped her? Or broke her?

Andy backed up so far that he fell into the rocker in the corner.

"Andy first," Mom said briskly, handing the baby to Dad. Dad carried the tiny bundle over to Andy and placed her carefully in his terrified arms. "Hold her close," Dad whispered.

Andy brought her to his chest and clutched her. He looked down at her and studied her puckered little face, then he relaxed and smiled.

"It's easy," he said, looking around at the others. "Who's next?"

The boys took turns holding her. Each was enthralled. She was so tiny and helpless. She needed them.

One by one, they held this new member of their family, and deep in their hearts, where they couldn't even see, each vowed to take care of her, protect her, and love her.

"What are we going to name her?" Davy asked. "I don't know any girl's names that start with "I".

"We'll skip 'I'," Mom said serenely. "We'll name her Jennifer Louise after my dear mother and Dad's dear mother. I wish they were still here. They would love her."

They took her home two days later. They had waited to celebrate Christmas until Mom and Jenny came home. They celebrated that first day. A neighbor had sent over a beautiful dinner so Mom could rest. After dinner, they opened gifts. Everyone was pleased. The last gift was from all the boys to Jenny, a soft brown bear with a pointy nose and brown bead eyes and movable arms and legs. He was almost as big as Jenny. Happy gently sat the bear in the corner of the bassinet. Strangely when Mom looked later in the evening, the bear was cuddled next to Jenny with her arm around it. Every night after that, she always found the bear in the same place, cuddled next to Jenny with her arm around it. They called the bear "Ted."

Theirs was a house full of boy things and just a few girl things, a girl toy from each of the boys bought at the drug store on the way to the hospital to bring Mom and Jenny home and a pink lace bassinette borrowed from a cousin. Dad placed the bassinette in his and Mom's bedroom next to Mom's side of their bed and stacked diapers under a changing table against the wall. There was a large diaper pail, and the boys had already added "Take out dirty diapers" to their chore lists. In the corner of the bedroom was a large bag of baby boy toys and clothes that would have to be exchanged after the holidays.

Life resumed in the Baxter household. The boys continued all the activities they had been doing and made time for Jenny. They were surprised that they looked forward to holding her, talking to her, playing with her, even rocking her. Mom did all the things she had been doing plus caring for Jenny. Dad went to work and hurried home each night to hold Jenny and give her a bottle. He said Jenny looked like a princess and started calling her "Princess." It became her nickname.

By the time spring came, even the boys' rowdy games included Princess. They would carefully take turns holding her as they threw baskets in the driveway and ran around the baseball diamond in the backyard. They took her with them in her little stroller when they went to the mall. She attracted a lot of attention from all the teenage girls, a definite plus. The eight Baxter kids were now nine.

Princess grew into a fearless one-year-old whose brothers vied for her attention and helped her learn to walk. By the time she was two, she ruled the household with her charm and wide-eyed sweetness. She was a giggly little girl who sadly waved goodbye to her brothers each morning when they left for school and sat by the window each afternoon waiting to welcome them home. As they walked through the door, she ran to them to be picked up and hugged. Each day they came home to sunshine.

Princess became an adventurous and confident three-year-old. She always felt safe and unafraid. She had eight protectors, after all.

And wherever she was, Ted was with her. She lost him all the time. She would set him down or throw him out of the shopping cart then cry when she couldn't see him anymore. Then the boys would have to find him. After a few times of searching for Ted, it became a game.

If Ted went missing, one of the boys would shout, "Ted's gone! The hunt is on!"

The boys would all link arms and search. They would run like a human wave around the store or church or park or backyard, heads down, looking around, weaving in and around people and counters and trees, down the store aisles, up the church aisles, around and around the park, shouting, "Find Ted! Where's Ted? Have you seen Ted?"

The brothers would search until they found Ted then present him to Princess, all of them bowing down and saying, "Here is Ted, dear Princess. He was lost, but your humble knights have found him again." Princess would giggle and hug Ted.

Sometimes people, especially children, would join them in the search. Once, in the grocery store, a little boy yanked Ted from the shopping cart and handed him to Gerdy. "Here is Ted for the princess!" he shouted. Gerdy accepted Ted and bowed to him then presented Ted to Princess. The little boy talked about it for days.

The Baxter brothers and their little Princess.

When Princess was three-and-a-half, the brothers came home from school to find their father sitting at the kitchen table, sobbing, tears running down his cheeks. The boys would have known something was wrong even if he hadn't been crying. Dad never came home early.

And where was Princess? And Mom?

They looked in her little bedroom but no Princess. They searched the house and the yard, no Princess. And no Mom.

It was a while before their father was able to stop crying and calm down enough to explain.

Princess and Mom were at the hospital. Mom had taken her in to see the doctor because she was so tired and pale lately. The doctor sent them to the hospital for tests. Mom had just called. Princess had cancer. Very bad cancer.

They all stared at each other, then Freddy asked, "Is she going to die?"

No one knew. Not yet.

"Is she going to stay in the hospital?"

"Can we go see her?"

Yes and yes. But they had to be calm and not start crying when they saw her. If they started crying, Princess would be scared.

"We don't know much yet," Dad said softly, "I will tell you as soon as I know. For now…"

They went to the hospital. When they got there, Mom repeated that they must not scare Princess by crying. If they felt crying coming on, they should say they had to go to the bathroom and run out of the room. They all nodded.

They were shocked to see Princess lying in the big bed. She looked so tiny and so pale. She had an IV in one arm and a blood pressure cuff on the other. She looked like she would start to cry at any moment.

Andy swallowed hard when he saw her then he took a deep breath and smiled. He walked over to the bed and bent over her.

"Hey, Princess," he said in a cheery voice, "What's happening? Where's Ted?"

Princess looked at Ted who was lying next to her. Andy followed her gaze and acted surprised to see Ted.

"Is Ted sick?" he asked.

Princess looked doubtfully at Ted then nodded.

A nurse was just coming into the room. Chris asked her, "Could you put a pressure cuff on Ted, please? The bear?"

The nurse glanced at all the boys crowded around the bed and smiled.

"Of course," she replied, "I'll get one."

She left the room and returned in a moment with a very small neo-natal pressure cuff. She wrapped it around Ted's small arm while Princess watched closely. Princess smiled when the nurse left the cuff on Ted.

The boys all talked excitedly to Princess and took turns reading to her. They were all waiting for the doctors to decide what to do. Then they were told the decision would not be made until the next day. Mom and Dad decided to stay at the hospital with Princess. Andy had a drivers' license and could drive the others home. Dad took money from his billfold and handed it to Andy to get some take-out food for dinner. To his surprise, Andy refused.

Andy insisted on staying there with them, with Princess. The other boys also insisted. They decided they could sleep on the floor just fine. They were a family, right? They were supposed to stick together, right? Mom and Dad gave in, partly because they were too worn to argue but mostly because the boys were right. They were a family, and they would stick together. And maybe they could make it through even this.

They took turns eating dinner in the hospital cafeteria. First, the boys went down, and Mom and Dad stayed with Princess, then Mom and Dad went down, and the boys stayed with Princess. Nobody ate very much.

The boys were in the way, and the nurses were constantly weaving around them and gently pushing them out of the way. But the nurses never asked them to leave or even frowned. They had never seen a family like this one before.

Having her brothers nearby helped Princess face all this or maybe just put it out of her mind. Whichever it was, it brought the color back to her cheeks, and she smiled. They told silly jokes and teased her and read children's books to her and when the nurse had to draw blood, Freddy lay down beside her and held her hand for the nurse to poke a finger.

Andy and Bri went home and brought back Princess's favorite DVDs and four sleeping bags. The hospital supplied the DVD player, and everyone watched *The Swan Princess* and *Cinderella* together until Princess fell asleep.

The boys slept on the floor on sleeping bags and Mom and Dad slept, when they slept at all, on a cot that was brought in. Throughout the night, the nurses checked on Princess, making their way around and over the boys sprawled on the floor. Sometimes, one of the brothers would be sitting on the edge of the bed holding Princess's hand or kneeling by the bed praying for her. The nurses threw light blankets over them and smiled and called nurses on other stations to tell them. Several stopped by to see this large family, eight brothers and a very tiny, very sick little sister.

The next day, the decisions were made. Princess could go home. But she would have to return regularly for chemotherapy. They were told the treatments would be hard on her and would make her nauseous and tired. But hopefully, it would kill the cancer. All ten of them listened quietly to everything the doctors said. The only thing the boys really remembered was that it would kill the cancer. It would be hard, and Princess would be sick, but it would kill the cancer. They held onto that thought like a beacon and took Princess home.

Princess went in regularly for treatments. Ted was always with her. Each time, one or five or all of her brothers went, too. They read to her and did what they could to get her to smile and tried to make this very difficult time easier for her.

When she got home, some of the boys were always with her. When she had trouble sleeping, one of her brothers would lie down beside her, and she would sleep cuddled up against his chest with his arms around her. Once, she threw up all over Bri's chest. He made a face and carefully eased out of bed. He got a wet washcloth and cleaned Princess's face. Then he took off his shirt, threw it in the laundry, washed his chest, put on a clean shirt, and laid down with Princess again.

Whenever she felt up to it, the brothers took her out of the house to the mall or the park or anywhere she wanted to go just like they always had. Princess loved it, and of course, Ted was always with her. She was weak most of the time and dropped Ted, or maybe she dropped him on purpose. She loved the game.

But now they took no chances of losing Ted. They watched Ted closely all the time. If he fell, one of the boys stayed with him while another shouted, "Ted's gone! The hunt is on!" The boys would all link arms and start searching, running like a human wave all around until they found him.

Sometimes, all they did on the outing was search for Ted. It made Princess laugh, so they didn't care. The Baxter brothers and Princess. Everyone knew who they were. And everyone knew how sick little Princess was. It got so that when they were searching for Ted now, people cheered and shouted, "The hunt is on! Find Ted!" It made Princess smile.

Princess's hair fell out, and her mom shaved her own head so she and Princess looked the same. The next day, Dad and the boys went to get groceries, and when they returned, they all had shaved heads. That made Princess laugh.

The boy's friends brought perfect fruit for Princess because she didn't have much of an appetite. They sent her princess coloring books and washable markers. One boy brought over his golden retriever, Goldie, for her to pet and ride on. Princess liked that.

When the chemotherapy was done, the doctors were very hopeful. The tests looked good but would have to be repeated in two months. They waited. Princess's hair started growing back. Mom and Dad and the boys were relieved to let their hair grow back.

Life went on. The boys continued to take her with them and read to her and play with her. Princess got her appetite back and ate more. She got stronger and played in the backyard on the swing and slide set by herself. Ted got lost and found almost every day. Everything was going great.

Then one day, Princess got a headache. It was so bad that she grabbed her head and fell down. They took her back to the hospital. The boys had a bad feeling and took off school to go to the appointment with her. They sat in the waiting room while the doctors did tests. When all was done, Mom and Dad brought Princess out. The boys looked into their parents' faces, and they knew. The cancer was back again. This time there was nothing the doctors could do. The cancer had spread everywhere. They told Princess she was coming home to rest and to get better. The boys forced smiles and teased her, and she believed them. She thought she was going home to live. They knew she wasn't.

The brothers did everything they could to make Princess happy in those last days. On good days, her brothers took her with them wherever they went. She went to hockey practice and basketball games. She went all the places they had always gone and to some new places like the zoo, the arboretum, the movie theater, and the library, where she got her own card and took out a book. They never returned the book. They paid for it and kept it. They wanted to show her as much as possible of the world while she was still with them.

They took turns sleeping on the floor next to her bed or holding her and cuddling her when she had trouble sleeping. She was never alone. And over and over they played the game of finding Ted. It was one of the few things that made her smile.

They hated and feared what was growing in her, the thing that was trying to destroy her, the cancer.

They were playing the game, searching for Ted in the backyard, holding hands, the human wave racing around the backyard, up and down the alley, around the house. Andy was carrying Princess while the others shouted and searched. Princess was giggling. Before they came outside, she had hugged each of them and Mom and Dad. She said, "I love you" to each of them. They didn't think anything of it. She often hugged them, and she often said, "I love you."

They knew where Ted was, next to the back door on the side of the step. Princess had dropped him coming out the door. When they finally got back to the step and picked him up, they presented him to Princess as they always did.

All of them bowed down and said, "Here is Ted, dear princess. He was lost, but your humble knights have found him again."

Andy was holding Princess and felt her weight press harder against his chest and her little body go limp. He looked down at her. Her eyes were closed.

"Princess?" he whispered.

She didn't answer, didn't respond. The other boys looked up. They all knew. The boys stood up silently and held the door open for Andy. He carried Princess in and went to the living room. Mom and Dad were both sitting on the couch reading the morning paper. They looked up and saw the silent tears running down Andy's face and Princess limp in his arms. All the boys were gathered around him. Andy kneeled and laid Princess on her mother's lap. The others kneeled around him. David was holding Ted. He reached over Andy and put Ted on Princess's right arm.

Ed whispered, "Is she…"

Dad listened to her chest and took her pulse then nodded. He started to cry quietly. Mom brought Princess's head up and kissed her face then held her close, slowly rocking back and forth. The boys stayed kneeling for a long time.

Finally, Dad said, "Let's pray for Princess."

They all reached out a hand and laid it wherever they could reach on Princess' shoulders, legs, hair, face.

Dad prayed. "Dear Lord, here is our Princess. We give her to you now. Please hold her close. Tell her we'll all join her someday. We miss her already. Amen."

Dad stood up and said, "I'd better call the hospice and tell them."

He left the room. Mom continued to rock back and forth. The boys stayed where they were.

When he returned, Dad said, "They said to put her in her bed. They won't come for a while. We can call anyone who might want to say goodbye to her. I should call them when we're ready for them to come and get her." He picked her up and carried her to her bed. Mom carried Ted, and the boys followed. When Princess was in her bed with Ted in her arms, Mom lay down and held her for a long time, her eyes closed.

"She should wear that silky green dress," Happy said softly, "She looks pretty in that dress."

"That's a good choice, Happy," Mom said. "Why don't you get it out of the closet."

"And you, David, pick out shoes for her. Ed, get pretty socks with lace on them. Gerdy, get a pink purse. Bri, pick a ribbon or a bow for her hair. Andy, get the bottle of pink nail polish. Chris, get her book of Bible stories. Freddy, look in her princess jewelry box. There is a necklace with a little angel on it."

Quickly, the boys gathered the things Mom requested and laid them at the foot of the bed. Then they all lay down on the floor, crying softly. After a bit, they fell asleep.

They woke when Judith, the hospice nurse came. The boys sat up and watched as she examined Princess and talked to Mom and Dad. She brought a small suitcase with her and put into it all the things lying on the end of the bed. She also took a picture from the nightstand. It was Princess holding Ted sitting on the picnic table with all her brothers around her. She was grinning.

"You can say goodbye now, boys." Judith had a soft voice.

One by one, they kissed Princess's cheek and said goodbye.

Dad carried Princess downstairs to Judith's car, and then she was gone.

Nobody talked much over the next three days. And then it was the day for the funeral.

All the boys wore dress pants and shirts and ties. Dad wore a suit and Mom wore a soft blue dress that Princess had especially liked. The church was only two blocks from their house. They arrived early and stood around while people came up to tell them how sorry they were and how much they liked or loved Princess. The boys said "Thank you" hundreds of times.

It was a nice service. The boys thought Princess would have liked it. Everyone sang "Jesus Loves Me" because it was Princess's favorite song. When the service ended, the eight brothers carried the small coffin down the center aisle to the hearse waiting outside.

Then they waited while the coffin was loaded. Mom and Dad stood by the waiting limousine.

"Where's Ted?" David asked looking around.

Mom looked up in alarm. "Ted isn't here? We forgot Ted?"

Dad shook his head. "We can't go looking for him now," he said. "Everyone is waiting."

Mom's voice rose heading for hysteria. "We can't bury her without Ted! We just can't!"

"No, we can't!" said Andy. He looked resolutely at his brothers then shouted, "Ted's gone! The hunt is on!"

The boys suddenly came to life. They linked arms and began running like a human wave around the hearse, through the parking lot, across the street and down the block. On they ran, through the park and down another block, heads down, looking around, weaving in and around people and parked cars and trees, shouting, "Find Ted! Where's Ted? Have you seen Ted?"

They raced down the street to their own house and around the house into the backyard, then into the house and up the stairs to Princess's room. They found Ted.

The brothers ran and fell down the stairs, out the back door and around to the front then down the street, all the while shouting, "We're coming, Princess. We found Ted." They ran like a human wave, arms linked, through the park, down the street and into the parking lot, shouting all the way, "We're coming, Princess. We found Ted."

Everybody was still in the parking lot, frowning and talking and shaking their heads. Mom and Dad had refused to leave without the boys. Dad was talking about going after them, but he didn't want to leave Mom. They heard the boys even before they saw them running, the human wave, with Freddy on one end waving Ted in the air.

When they came around the hearse, they all stopped, breathing hard. They stood for a moment catching their breath. No one said anything. Everyone stared at the brothers.

Then Freddy stepped forward and bowed in front of the casket.

"Here is Ted, dear Princess," he said softly.

All the boys bowed in front of the casket.

"He was lost," Freddy continued, "but your humble knights have found him again."

It was silent for a moment, then Freddy stood up and gently laid Ted on top of the coffin. Then he walked over to the limo past his Mom and Dad and climbed in.

The other boys stood, and one by one, they came to the coffin, picked up Ted, bowed, and repeated what Freddy had said then laid Ted on top of the coffin again.

"Here is Ted, dear Princess. He was lost, but your humble knights have found him again."

When the last boy was in the limo, Mom and Dad climbed in too.

The coffin was opened, and Ted was placed inside. Princess would never again lose her Ted.

When love stands up and shines, you can't miss it. Everyone who was there watching saw love shining. It made them cry. And smile.

The boys were finally at peace. The humble knights would have to continue without their Princess, but they would never forget her. Each of them would tell this fairytale to his children and his children's children. He would tell of the magical, beautiful princess and her best friend, Ted. He would tell of the knights who searched and found Ted and rescued him and brought him back, time after time, to his beloved princess. And in the telling, their children would learn about love and maybe, just maybe, someday, they would stand up in love and shine. For their own prince or princess—in their own fairytale.

THE EMPTY CHAIR

She stood looking out the window. Jack had just come in from work. He barely made it home because the snow had turned into a blizzard. She could hardly see to the end of the driveway. She felt Timmy tugging on her skirt.

"Where Dan?" he asked. "Want play him."

Marisa closed her eyes and sighed. *When will he stop asking?* she thought. *It's been four weeks.*

"He's with Jesus, now. Remember? We went to church, and we all prayed for him. He's in Heaven, Timmy. He isn't coming home anymore. Remember?"

"Oh, okay." Timmy walked away. A moment later he returned.

"Mommy, where Dan? Want talk him."

She turned around and looked down at her toddler. The same question over and over. She just couldn't make him understand.

"He's with Jesus, Timmy," she patiently explained again. "He's in Heaven. He isn't coming home anymore. Remember?"

"Oh, okay." He turned away.

More to distract him, she said, "Time for dinner, dear. Go wash up."

"Oh, okay," he replied. He started down the hall to the bathroom.

She closed her eyes when she heard the wheel squeaking. He was pushing Dan's wheelchair into the kitchen. Just as he did for every meal. And after the meal, he would push it back into his own room and leave it right next to his bed. So it would be there when Dan came home.

She watched him push the wheelchair to the table. He patted the seat and said smiling, "Dan."

She wiped her tears so he wouldn't see them and smiled back, nodding. *Will he ever understand?* she wondered.

Dinner was ready. She called Jack, and they all sat at the table, trying to ignore the empty chair. She and Jack talked a bit about his day at work and her day with the kids. Timmy sat in the chair next to the wheelchair. He leaned left toward the wheelchair, his arm resting on its tray, and ate with his right hand. When Dan was still here, he sat like that and put food on Dan's tray, even though Dan couldn't pick it up. His illness had robbed him of muscle strength, and he had to be spoon fed. She could see him sitting there next to her, waiting patiently, smiling at everyone, and laughing at his little brother. She closed her eyes then got up and went to the far counter and got a tissue. She stood there wiping her tears and her nose, calming herself. She couldn't just go off and cry all the time, she reminded herself. She had a family to care for. *Timmy misses him so much*, she thought. *I do too.*

Crash! Screech! Screech! Bang! Bang!

"What was that?" Marisa shouted, rushing to the window. "Oh, Jack, two cars crashed! Right under the street light at the corner. One of them is on fire. A woman is trying to get out. We've got to help them."

She grabbed her coat from the hook and opened the door. The frigid air hit her face. She could hardly see through the swirling snow. Jack yanked her back inside. "Get your boots," he yelled as he ran out the door, his coat open, his boots unzipped.

She put her boots on and grabbed her hat and gloves. "Stay inside," she yelled at Timmy, then ran out the door, slamming it behind her.

A van and a small pickup had collided. The driver door of the van was partly open and bent. Jack was trying to pull a woman out, but the door wouldn't open further. He could see flames on the far side of the van from under the hood. They were growing larger, shooting up the sides of the hood. Very soon, they would be inside the van.

Jack pulled her arms, and the woman finally squeezed out through the damaged door and fell to the ground. "Help him! Help him!" she screamed then fainted. She had a large bump on her forehead.

Jack looked toward the pickup. The two vehicles were crumpled together. The driver's side of the pickup was smashed into the van's passenger side. A man was emerging from the pickup's passenger door. The pickup's driver side window was open, and the flames were leaping from the van through that window into the pickup.

The man took a step, screamed in pain, and fell to the ground clutching his knee.

The flames were growing higher. The smoke made it hard to see. Jack started to drag the woman away from the car. Marisa had run down the steps and now grabbed the woman's feet and waved Jack to help the man. The snow was coming down so thick it was hard to distinguish snow from smoke.

"Mommy!" Timmy yelled as he ran down the steps to her. Marisa looked up. The front door was wide open, and Timmy was running in his stocking feet with no coat.

"Timmy!" she screamed. "Get back in the house!"

Timmy pointed at the van.

"Mommy, Mommy, boy. Help! Get!"

Marisa turned toward the burning van, her face puzzled. Suddenly, she understood! The woman had said help him. She didn't mean the other driver, she meant her son, her child, in the car—the burning car! He must be in the back seat. Marisa stared. She could barely see him through the smoke.

The woman on the ground was moaning but appeared to be unconscious. Marisa stared at the car for a moment then jumped up. "Jack," she screamed. "There's a boy in the back seat. We've got to get him out!"

"Timmy, get Mommy's phone. Call 911. Can you do that?" Timmy nodded. "Tell them the cars are on fire, and people are hurt. Then bring the phone to Mommy. Don't hang up!"

"Oh, okay." Timmy ran back to the house.

Jack had helped the man to the curb away from the vehicles. Now, he ran to the burning van and tried to open the side door. It wouldn't open. He could barely see the boy through the smoke. He was in a wheelchair. He tried the tailgate, but it wouldn't open either.

The electric is burned, he thought. He reached around through the driver's smashed door to manually unlock the side door. I can't get the lock up. Maybe if I pull up the handle...

He strained his arm but couldn't reach the handle through the narrow opening. Marisa pushed him aside and tried, but she couldn't reach either. She looked back at the woman lying on the ground. The woman was very small and slender. Otherwise, she would have also been trapped. She could hear the boy now, crying out in fear. There was nothing they could do. She stepped back, and she and Jack joined hands and began praying for a miracle to get the boy out.

"Door open, Mommy."

Marisa looked up, shocked. Timmy was standing inside the burning car holding out her cell phone. He was smiling and patting the boy's hand. The flames were coming into the front seat now. Marisa grabbed Timmy out of the car, and Jack unhooked the boy, no bigger than Dan, and lifted him out of the wheelchair. Jack carefully sat down in the doorway then stepped down from the van carrying the boy. They all backed away from the burning van. The pickup was burning now, too.

Marisa grabbed the phone.

"Are you there? This is the 911 operator. Are you still there, Timmy?"

"This is Timmy's mom." Marisa could hardly get the words out. Then she said to Timmy, "Go in the house, Timmy. We'll be right there. Stay in the house."

"This is Timmy's mom," Marisa repeated.

"Oh," the operator said speaking very fast, "It was hard to understand Timmy, but I could make out a few words, uh, cars, fire, Dabid and…." Then she took a deep breath and said, "Fire trucks and paramedics are on their way." She paused. "I think Timmy was saying you got the two drivers out, but a boy was still in the back seat and couldn't get out. Is he still in there?"

"No," Marisa whispered, "He's out." *Thanks to Timmy*, she thought.

They could hear the fire sirens. They sounded very far away.

"Jack, will the cars explode?" Marisa suddenly asked.

"I don't know," he answered. "But we've got to get everyone away from them."

Jack ran toward the house and up the ramp with the boy in his arms. Timmy was watching at the window and opened the door. Jack looked around to see where to lay the boy.

"Dabid," Timmy said.

Jack turned around. Timmy had pushed the wheelchair over to him. "Dabid," he repeated, patting the seat.

Jack sat the boy in the wheelchair and buckled the seat belt. He stared at the boy for a moment. *He's just the size Dan was*, he thought. Then he gulped back a sob and took a deep breath.

"Watch him, Tim," he said. Timmy nodded.

Jack ran out the door. The fire sirens were closer now. Two neighbors had come out to help. Together, Jack and one neighbor carried the unconscious woman into the house and laid her on the floor. Timmy ran and got a blanket and covered her and pushed a pillow under her head. "Mommy okay, Dabid," he said to the boy in the wheelchair.

Marisa and the other neighbor were carrying the man. Jack took Marisa's place, and she hurried ahead of them. She was surprised to see the woman was covered and the boy was in the wheelchair. She ran for more blankets and a pillow. They covered the man and sent Timmy for another pillow to brace the man's leg.

A few minutes later, the fire engines arrived, and paramedics and equipment filled the living room. Jack was sitting at the kitchen table watching, still wearing his jacket and boots. His face was red and sooty. Timmy stood shyly in the doorway watching.

A shock of frigid air swept in as a fireman stepped in through the front door. "The fire is out. We'll stay for a few minutes more to be sure. We opened both hoods and all the doors and trunks and sprayed it all."

Timmy had turned when the door opened. He looked at the fireman, then he looked over at the wheelchair. He frowned and went over to the wheelchair. The boy was crying, but there was no sound. Tears streamed down his cheeks. Timmy patted his hand.

"Okay," he said softly, "Mommy okay. Mommy sleep. Dabid okay." Timmy smiled at the boy, then he climbed up on a chair and leaned toward him from the side, resting his head against the other boy's head. "Okay," he said. "Dabid okay."

The boy stopped crying and closed his eyes.

One of the paramedics came out to talk to them. "It looks like they'll be okay. We'll take them to the hospital, but they should be fine. The boy, too. He breathed in a bit of smoke but doesn't seem to be too bothered. I'm going to enjoy writing this report, thanks to you guys. You saved their lives."

The fireman said, "Great! I've got to get back outside." He walked over to Jack and Marisa. "I want to shake your hand, sir. That was very brave, pulling those people out of the fire."

"My wife helped too," Jack mumbled. The fireman shook Marisa's hand then smiled and turned to the door to leave.

"Wait," Jack called. "We're not the heroes. It was Timmy. He called 911. He was the one who climbed into the burning car and opened the back door while we were praying. He covered them up when we brought them in. He brought Danny's wheelchair over for the boy.

"Dabid," Timmy said. He patted the boy's hand. "He Dabid."

Everyone stared at Timmy. The fireman stood staring for several seconds, then he cleared his throat and walked over to Timmy. He put out his hand. Timmy backed up.

"It's okay, Timmy," Jack said. "I think he wants to shake your hand."

"Oh, okay." Timmy put his hand out, and the fireman shook it.

"You are a very brave young man. A real hero." He smiled, reached out and tousled Timmy's hair then went out the door.

When they were all stable, the paramedics took them out to the ambulances. They reassured the boy that his mom would be fine, and Timmy held his hand until they left.

As the paramedic was going out the door, he turned to Jack. "You should bring your son to the hospital tomorrow. Introduce these people to their hero."

The next morning, Marisa called the hospital. All three were stable. John Mason, the pickup driver, was awaiting knee surgery. Mrs. Kintso was awake, and she and her son were anxious to see them.

Jack and Marisa stood in the open garage door watching as the burned cars were being removed. The storm had stopped sometime during the night, but the air still seemed smoky. Timmy was already in the car and watched through the back window.

Jack and Marisa climbed into the van. They both stopped when they saw the wheelchair in the back already hooked in and ready to go. Tim smiled at them and patted the seat of the wheelchair.

"Dabid," he said.

Jack opened his mouth to speak then sighed and shook his head instead.

At the hospital, Tim insisted on taking the chair in. "Dabid," he said.

When they reached Mrs. Kintso's room, the boy saw Timmy and grinned and made happy sounds. He was sitting in a hospital wheelchair that was much too big for him.

Timmy pushed the wheelchair over to him and patted the boy's hand. "Hi, Dabid." He pulled the boy's hand over to touch the wheelchair. "Dabid."

The boy nodded and grinned looking at his mother. Mrs. Kintso smiled then looked puzzled.

"Have we met before? "How do you know my son's name?"

"I don't think we've met," Marisa responded. "Timmy must have heard it from the firemen or paramedics."

"But, he couldn't have. My purse was burned. Everything in the car was burned, David's wheel-chair..." she paused. "Even the license plate was burned. They couldn't identify us or the van. No one knew who we were until I woke up sometime during the night." She touched her bandaged forehead. "I have a concussion, but I'll be okay," she explained.

She paused again and wiped away a tear. "Thank God, David got out okay!"

Timmy spoke up, "Danny. Chair Dabid. Take." He patted David's hand. "Dabid chair."

Mrs. Kentso stared at him.

"Timmy," she said slowly, "who told you his name? He can't talk."

"Danny."

"Tim," Marisa interrupted. "Danny is in Heaven."

Timmy nodded, "Danny Jesus. Danny gone. Danny chair. Dabid chair."

Timmy grinned, and David did, too.

Mrs. Kentso turned to David.

"Did you see Danny?"

David nodded vigorously.

Marisa sat up straighter and leaned forward. "Tim, Danny said the chair is for David?"

Tim nodded, "Dabid."

Marisa smiled. "Then it is. This is your chair now, David. Bless you."

Tim patted David's hand, and both boys grinned.

"Mrs. Kentso," Marissa continued," Christmas is in two days. We would love for you and David to join us if you can. And David is welcome to stay with us if he is ready to leave before you. Or you can both come. We have room."

"Dabid friend. Danny like. Tim like."

"Is Danny still here, Tim?" Jack asked.

Tim shook his head. "Danny Jesus. Danny no sick. Danny gone. Bye, Danny."

The snow had started again, soft flakes falling slowly and gently. Everyone looked out the window and thought of miracles. Timmy and David just smiled.

EVERGREENS AND LITTLE BOYS

SLAM!

Janet jumped as the door to the garage slammed. She could hear the garage door opening. She ran to the front window and saw Barry's car backing out very fast then screeching as he slammed on the brakes, stopping barely in time to miss hitting a car driving past. The tires squealed as the car lurched backward into the street then abruptly jerked forward. He never looked at the house and didn't close the garage door.

She blinked a tear. First the heart attack, then COPD. Now, he tired easily. It slowed him down and made him angry. This morning, when he misdialed the house phone and got a wrong number, he was so angry, he yanked the phone from the wall and threw it across the room.

The worst part was he knew he did it to himself. All the years of smoking had finally caught up with him.

They had always had a happy marriage. But now she had no idea what to do. If only he would talk.

She stood at the window a long time, lost in her thoughts. Suddenly, a movement to the left of the driveway caught her attention. She looked closer. It was just a car parking in front of her mailbox. The mail was due in about an hour. She wondered if she should go out and ask them to back up the car.

Then she thought, *Does it really matter?* She started to turn away then looked back as both front doors opened. She didn't recognize either of the men getting out. The driver came around the back of the car. He opened the trunk, poked around inside, then closed it again. At that moment, she thought she saw an arm stick out, a very small arm. She shook her head. *That's ridiculous*, she thought. *My imagination is working overtime. I should go get a cup of coffee.* She continued watching.

The other man opened the passenger-side back door. He leaned in. Through the car's front window, she could barely see him. She blinked her eyes. Again, it looked like an arm sticking up. It looked like the man's arm was pushing down the small arm—or whatever it was. It looked like the man's arm swept halfway across the back seat and back again, very fast, almost like he struck something. She blinked again. What was happening in that car?

The man stood up and closed the door. The two men talked for a minute, then the driver pointed past her driveway down the street. The other man nodded, and they walked briskly away. She could see now that the driver was carrying a gas can. *They must have run out of gas*, she thought. She laughed slightly. Mystery solved.

She was starting to turn away from the window when she saw something moving in the back seat. It was a warm day. It looked like all the windows were up in the car, and the car was sitting in the sun. She didn't stick her nose in other people's business, but if there was a dog in the car... It was just over a mile to the gas station. She thought a moment then ran out through the garage and down to the car.

She was not prepared for what was in the back seat. She looked through the side window and saw three little boys, maybe four or five years old, buckled into seat belts with their hands tied! One of the boys had worked one hand out of the rope knot. He looked up at her and yelled. She couldn't make out what he said, but obviously he needed help. She tried the door. It was locked. She tried the other doors, but they were all locked.

"Call the police," she said aloud.

She turned to go back to the house to call, then she heard tapping. She looked back and saw the boy twisting to reach the lock button. It seemed to be too far. She could only watch as he twisted and strained and finally got two fingers over and flipped the button up. He got it!

She opened the door, and the boy started crying, then the other two boys started crying. She helped him pull his other hand from the knot, and he unbuckled his seat belt.

"Unbuckle him!" She pointed at the boy in the middle then reached inside and pulled up the driver's door lock. She slammed the car door and ran around the car to the other rear door. She unbuckled the third boy, and all three climbed out of the car.

"We'll untie in the house," she said, pointing at the open garage door. The second and third boys ran up the driveway. The first boy was trying to open the trunk. She tried to pull him away until he yelled, "There's two more in there!"

The trunk was locked. She ran around to the driver's door. She opened the door and looked for a lever or button to open the trunk. She found it near the floor by the door. She pulled the lever, and the trunk started opening. She could hear the boy yelling, "Hurry! Get out quick!"

Two more boys tumbled out of the trunk. Their hands were also tied. All three boys ran up the driveway.

She looked down the street and prayed they would all be safely in the house before the men returned. She closed the trunk and hit the driver's lock button, then slammed the door and ran up the driveway. As soon as she got into the garage, she pushed the wall button to close the garage door. All of them held their breath until the door was all the way down. Then the boys started talking loudly.

"Shhh!" she whispered.

The boys froze and stared at her. They looked terrified. She opened the door to the house, and they all piled in, pushing and shoving. Once inside, she took them to the kitchen, got a pair of scissors, and cut the ropes off their wrists. As each boy was freed, he went soundlessly to the front window, head lowered, watching the car.

I've got to call the police, she thought. She picked up the house phone, but there was still no dial tone.

She would have to use a neighbor's phone. But all her neighbors worked; no one was home during the day. Barry had been urging her for several years to get a cell phone. She refused. She told him she didn't want a cell phone, didn't need one—but she sure wished she had one now.

"Mum!" the boys all turned to her wide-eyed as they slid down the wall to the floor. Over their heads, through the window, she could see the men approaching the car, stopping when they realized the boys were gone. They peered around at all the houses searching for a sign of the boys. Suddenly, the driver went behind the car and opened the trunk. She could see his face, his mouth moving angrily. They looked up at her house, and she held her breath. It was late afternoon, so with no lights turned on and the sheer curtains on the front window, they couldn't see inside. The driver pointed at her driveway. The other man shook his head and pointed down the street to the left. They talked for a minute then turned and went down the street, walking very slowly, staring at the houses trying to see into the backyards.

The children and Janet all exhaled at the same time. She chuckled, and the boys relaxed slightly and smiled.

One boy, the smallest was staring at the kitchen counter. Janet followed his gaze. There was a bowl of fruit on the counter.

"Are you guys hungry?" she asked.

They all nodded.

"Sit at the table, and I'll fix you something to eat."

The boys hurried to the table, noisily pulled out chairs and climbed up, then turned expectantly toward her. She smiled and brought the bowl of fruit to the table. Each boy took something. As they ate the fruit, she got bread, lunchmeat, cheese, and mayo, and quickly made sandwiches. She poured milk and brought the sandwiches and milk to the table. The children ate ravenously, then sat back in their chairs and sighed.

"My name is Janet. What are your names? How old are you?"

The oldest boy was the one who unlocked the car door. The boys seemed to look at him as the leader. His name was Tommy Pershing, and he was five and a half. John Benson was five; his brother Mikey was four. Mark Fairing was four, and Pedro Sanchez would be four next month. They didn't know each other before the men took them yesterday. None of them was sure what their address or phone was. They only knew they lived in the city.

"Across the river," Tommy added.

While they were eating, Tommy was watching the window. Suddenly, he said in a whisper, "They're back."

Everyone turned. The men had returned to the car. They poured the gas into the gas tank and put the can in the trunk. The driver talked on a cell phone. The other man again pointed at Janet's house. This time, the driver nodded, and they started up the driveway. The kids all slid off their chairs and hid behind the kitchen counter. Janet ran to the door to the garage and locked it. A moment later, they could all hear the doorknob on that door rattling as someone turned the knob and tried to come in. Janet stood next to the door, holding her breath. The rattling stopped.

The exterior doors were always kept locked, but Janet crept on hands and knees over to the front door and checked. It was locked.

Now that knob turned. The men were at the front door trying to see through the front window and the decorative glass in the front door. The doorbell rang, and everyone was startled.

The kids were all watching from the corner of the counter, their hands over their mouths to keep from talking. Mark was desperately trying not to cry. When he whimpered, the other boys glared at him. He covered his face with his arms. His shoulders shook, but there was no sound.

Janet was sitting on the floor against the wall a few feet from the front door. She was afraid she would be seen if she crossed to the kitchen. She was watching Tommy. He looked at her and held up his hand, palm toward her to indicate stop, then he stared at the door. Suddenly, he waved at her to come. She crawled to the counter and scooted behind it.

It was quiet now. The men must have left. Then they heard a new noise. Someone was running up the back outside stair to the deck. Where they were, they would be visible through the sliding doors to the deck. She waved at the boys to follow her. Soundlessly, they all moved over to and down the stairs. They stayed in the hallway to the family room. They could not be seen here. Suddenly, overhead, they heard the crash of breaking glass, then men talking. *They'll search upstairs first then down here*, she thought wildly. *They'll find us! We've got to run!*

As she thought it, she waved to the kids to follow her and went as fast as she could across the family room, unlocked the patio door, and they all went out. She closed the door carefully, quietly. Then she whispered, "Run!"

The boys ran. Janet held back at first to be sure none of them fell or faltered. The boys never looked back. They ran straight into the evergreen woods behind the house. In less than a minute, they were hidden. Then she took the lead. She knew where the two ponds were. They were well hidden with evergreens and tall grass around the edges, easy to fall into. She knew they were making noise while they were running, but it couldn't be helped. She just hoped the two men didn't hear it.

Suddenly, she heard a shout. She looked back. She could just see the deck and the two men pointing into the woods. The men moved out of view, and she knew they had been seen. The men were crashing through the woods now, shouting.

The boys stopped and looked back, frozen with fear. What should she do? Looking straight back toward the house, she suddenly realized the woods were much thicker on the left side. The smaller but deeper pond was in that area, too. She started moving sideways and waved the boys to follow her. They all came except Mark. He didn't move, just stared at the bushes being moved aside as the men came closer.

She caught Tommy's arm and whispered to him where to go, hoping they would all be safe. The boys started running with Tommy leading. Janet prayed Tommy would remember all the instructions and they would make it to safety. Then, she turned back and scooped up Mark, throwing him over her shoulder so she would still have an arm free to push through the thickening brush.

The shouts grew softer, and she knew the two men were still heading straight across the woods. When she heard a splash followed by much loud swearing, she laughed silently. The pond had claimed a victim. Yay! It was a relatively shallow pond, but it would slow them down. She did not slow down. She had to catch up with the boys. When she couldn't carry Mark anymore, she stopped and set him on the ground.

"Can you run now?" she asked gently.

Mark hugged her and nodded.

"He's so little," she thought, taking his hand. They walked for a while. She was exhausted. He didn't cry, but he hung on very tightly to her hand. She had warned Tommy about the second pond and told him to wait there for a little while for her and Mark. She had also told him where to go if she didn't make it. When she and Mark reached the pond, she didn't see the boys. *They've gone on*, she thought. *How will I find them now?*

A moment later, the boys appeared. They heard her coming and hid in case it was the men. Now what?

They all sat quietly for a few minutes. They had run a long way, and all were exhausted. While they rested, she asked them what had happened. How did they come to be in the car?

The boys didn't know much. They were taken and tied and thrown into the car. Tommy said it had happened yesterday. None of them knew why but each told her how he was taken.

Tommy was taken first. He was at the playground with friends. They were playing ball. The ball went into the woods, and Tommy ran to get it. When he reached down for the ball, a man grabbed him and carried him to the car. Tommy had a little brother, Noah, who was two. He was glad Noah wasn't there.

Then they drove around and saw Pedro walking down the street. The car stopped, and the driver rolled down his window and asked where the church was. Pedro came over to the car, and while he was explaining and pointing, the other guy got out, came around the car, and grabbed him. He pushed him in back and climbed in with him. He tied his hands and buckled him in and put clear tape over his mouth just like Tommy. Tommy said that's what they did to everyone.

John and Mikey were crossing the street. They saw the driver drop a jar of quarters. It broke on the sidewalk and quarters rolled all over. Both the men started picking up the quarters. They told John and Mikey if they helped pick them up, they would give each of them two dollars. When the boys got close, they grabbed them. They put John inside the car and Mikey in the trunk 'cause the car was full.

Mark was lost in a store, and the driver said he would help him find his mom. He told Mark his mom had gone out to their car to look for him. Mark went out with the man and was put in the trunk, too. Mark cried a lot at first. He banged on the trunk lid. When they opened it, Mark couldn't breathe very well because of the tape over his mouth and his crying. They took the tape off both the boys in the trunk. Then Pedro started crying and choking, so they took the tape off all of the boys if they promised not to talk at all. They promised. Nobody choked anymore.

Janet looked up. The small patch of sky they could still see was turning from blue to gray. Janet knew they could easily lose their way once it got dark. This dense part of the woods would be pitch dark soon. She tried to decide which way to go from here. She was pretty sure about the direction they had come from, but she didn't want to backtrack. The two men might still be out there. They had to get out of the woods to a street or someone's backyard and get help.

If I go this direction, she thought, *the woods will end at a street not that far from my house. I think. If I go that way, it would be bad. The woods extend that way for miles, ending*, she thought, *at a freeway with a high, chain-link barrier fence.* She sighed. The trouble was she had never exited the woods in either of those directions before. The only way she was sure of was back the way they had come.

The more she thought, the more confused and unsure she was. The boys were getting fidgety. It was getting dark, and they were all afraid of being in the woods at night. She mentally flipped a coin then said confidently, "We go this way."

As they started out, Janet prayed over and over, *Please, Lord, make this the right way.*

They walked until they were too tired to go any further. Janet let them rest for ten minutes then said, "Let's go."

When they refused to get up, she ruthlessly threatened to leave them there and started walking. They dragged themselves up and followed. An hour later, they stopped again because the children were falling asleep walking and crumpling to the ground. They had all done all they could. She dragged them all closer together under a big tree. She watched them shivering as they slept, their light jackets providing little warmth. She was wearing a t-shirt top and no jacket. She was shivering, too, as she sat on the ground leaning against a tree. And then she was asleep.

When Barry returned home that evening, Janet wasn't there. He called her name coming in from the garage. The house was dark. When he turned on the lights, he saw the broken sliding door, broken from the outside, glass all over in the house. Someone had broken in! He grabbed the house phone on the counter. No dial tone. Still not working. He dialed 911 on his cell phone then turned and saw the table, six plates and five glasses, chairs pulled out, food, and the half-empty fruit bowl. Who was here? Where was Janet? He looked back at the broken door and the evergreen woods beyond. What happened here?

"This is the 911 operator."

"I just got home from work. Someone broke into the house, the door to the deck is broken, glass is all over the dining room, and my wife is missing."

"Police are on their way. Please stay on the line until they arrive."

"I will."

He went to the front door and opened it. He switched on the outside lights and stared out at the street. Where was she? Was she all right? What if she never came back? She had to come back so he could tell her he was sorry, they could be okay again, handle this COPD thing together. He blinked at the headlights.

"They're here."

"You may hang up now, sir. Good luck."

Janet woke, hearing voices and smelling dirt. She opened her eyes. She was lying on her back, looking up, and five small faces were looking down at her. She shook her head and sat up. Where? What?

Then she remembered and got to her feet. She opened her arms, and all five boys ran over to hug her and be hugged. *They are so brave*, she thought, *and they believe that I will save them. I've got to save them, Lord!*

She looked over their heads, trying to figure out which way to go. "Okay, kids," she said, "We need to get going." The children all nodded, and Tommy walked over to the left of the tree. The others lined up behind him. *Is that the right way, Lord?* she wondered. Then she smiled, remembering the Bible verse, "And a little child shall lead them."

"Lead the way, Tommy," she called, and the march began.

By mid-morning, they were all tired and hungry. Tommy saw the berries and stuffed them into his mouth before she got there. The other boys did the same. She could only pray they wouldn't make the kids sick. Their faces were purple, and they were smiling when they sat down on the ground. Janet sat on a log and slowly munched the berries from the branch Mark had broken off and brought to her. They sure tasted good.

Sitting quietly, Janet suddenly heard a noise coming from up ahead. What was it? The boys heard it too.

Tommy said, "That's a car!"

They all stood up and started walking then running toward the sound. It wasn't far away. A dirt road! The boys all started cheering. The car noise stopped for a moment then started getting louder again.

"They're coming back," Mark yelled. "We'll get a ride."

They watched the car coming. As it came closer, the cheering stopped.

"Oh, no!" Janet whispered. "It's them. It's them! Run!"

The children scattered into the woods. They saw Janet through the trees and ran to her. She went into the woods a short way then pushed her way into a dense evergreen grove.

"Stay here," she whispered. "I'll draw them away, then I'll double back, and we'll head the other way on the other side of the road. Peek and see where they are, and sneak across the road when you can."

The boys all nodded except Tommy, who figured he had a better idea.

Janet carefully pushed out of the grove and quietly moved away from the grove and the searching men. One of the men saw her and shouted. Both men started running after her. She ran as fast as she could, but she knew they would eventually catch her. *It will be worth it if the boys can get away*, she thought. *Help, Lord!*

When the men were well past the grove, Tommy said, "Come on!" and ran in the other direction. They could hear the car engine. It was in the middle of the road with the doors open and the engine running. Tommy climbed into the driver's seat and closed the door. The other boys stood in the road. Was Tommy crazy?

"Get in, quick!" Tommy whispered. "Close the front door. Everybody in back!"

The confused boys did as he said. Tommy pushed down the door lock as soon as the boys were in the car.

They were still pulling the back door closed when the car started moving. Tommy was kneeling on one knee on the seat, leaning forward over the steering wheel, his other leg hanging down, his foot barely reaching the gas pedal. The car lurched forward with Tommy stepping on and off the gas pedal.

They passed the two men. The car was swerving back and forth on the dirt road with Tommy barely moving the steering wheel just trying to stay on the road. The men started running down the road after the car.

Janet was at the edge of the road when she saw the car coming. She turned to run into the wood when the horn honked, and the driver door opened. She stared and saw the many small arms waving from the back seat. Tommy stepped hard on the gas, then lifted his foot and placed it over the brake. When the car reached Janet, Tommy stomped on the brake, throwing all the boys forward and back. Tommy hung onto the steering wheel and yelled at Janet to get in the driver's side. All the boys yelled and pointed. The car slowed but didn't stop.

Janet ran to the driver door and jumped in, hanging onto the rim above the door and the back of the seat. Tommy jumped out of her way. She got onto the seat sideways and grabbed the steering wheel. The car lurched left. The men were almost up to the car. When it lurched, they jumped back, afraid of being hit. The car lurched right, and the door slammed shut when Janet twisted in the seat to face forward. She pushed down the lock button then stepped on the gas.

As she drove, she was so concentrated on getting away, she didn't register a car coming toward her. She didn't see it pass the two men and then do a U-turn. She didn't see it stop and offer the men a ride. And she didn't see the men climb in.

She drove about two miles and stopped at a gas station. Janet ran in and called 911 on the store phone. Then she called Barry's cell. It went directly to voice mail. *He must have turned it off,* she thought.

The police arrived very quickly. She told them a short version of events and described the two men who were walking on that road.

A minute later, Barry saw Janet standing next to the police car and drove into the gas station—with the two men in the car. Janet looked up and saw Barry, then recognized the two men getting out.

"That's them. That's the men!" she shouted.

Two more police cars were driving into the parking lot and all the officers converged on the surprised kidnappers.

The gas station manager recognized the boys from the Amber Alerts on television. He couldn't do enough for them. He brought coffee to Janet and Barry and loaded the kids with drinks, food, snacks, and bananas. The kids ate everything in sight. Their pictures would be on all the news programs that night, and the front page of the newspapers tomorrow. The kids were celebrities.

Everyone was taken to the police station. The boys hung onto Janet until their parents arrived. They told everyone Janet saved them. She was their hero! Janet couldn't stop praising the kids and telling everyone how brave, resourceful, and unbeatable they had been. Tommy was everyone's hero. He had never been in the driver's seat before, but he had listened to his father explaining how things worked and watched him drive and remembered.

The police chief came out of his office and praised and congratulated everyone.

Each of the children gave a statement for the record then went home with their parents.

Janet and Barry stayed longer, hoping the two men would explain why they took the children.

Andy Peterson and Terry Smith had long records starting in junior high school, including theft, burglary, and break-ins. It was never anything violent, and they never physically hurt anyone. They pretty much just took things that weren't theirs.

This time, though, they decided to expand their operations. A friend made a comment that little kids would make great drug runners. Nobody would suspect a little kid. The two thought it was a great idea. We'll get some kids and sell them to a local drug dealer. They didn't talk to the drug dealer first. He would have told them they were idiots. They just jumped up and did it.

Now, faced with kidnapping charges, they sat in their cells, crying and blaming each other.

Finally, they were alone, in their car, ready to go home. Barry sat staring at the steering wheel. "I'm so sorry, Janet," he said softly.

Janet looked at him then started crying. "Oh, Barry, if I had just listened to you and gotten a cell phone, I could have called the police right away. None of this would have happened!"

Barry stared at her for a moment then reached across and opened the glove compartment. He took out a small package and handed it to her.

"I bought this, and I was going to give it to you yesterday morning. But then I got mad and broke the house phone and stomped out the door..." He looked down, and she could hear the gulp in his throat. She had never seen him cry before.

"You could have been... I love you so much. I'm so sorry. Please forgive me. If those guys had caught you..."

Janet opened the package and smiled. "You got me a cell phone!"

He nodded. "I charged it, so you can use it right away. I wish I had given it to you yesterday."

Janet reached over and patted his hand. "Thank you," she said softly.

Barry stared out the window. Suddenly he blurted out," You are so brave! You saved those kids!"

He closed his eyes and his face revealed the anguish he felt. His face was pinched with regret. His voice was angry, "I am so worthless anymore. I just can't do anything right. I should have been there for you," he said softly. "I should have been there."

Janet stared at her husband then she grabbed his arm and shouted, "Barry, You caught the kidnappers! They would have gotten away! You stopped them! You're a hero!"

Barry stared at her, "I am?" he asked.

"Yes, you are. You've always been _my_ hero."

He put his hand over hers. "I'm so sorry, Janet. I'll never act like that again. I couldn't live without you."

"I couldn't live without you, either. I love you, Barry." She leaned over and kissed his cheek. "Let's go home now."

It was silent in the car. Then he nodded, smiling, and said, "The super heroes will now fly, oops, uh no, they'll drive home." They both laughed. "You and me, Janet."

"Yes!" Janet whispered, "You and me."

PEACHES

"Papa, Papa! Look at the peaches! Wow! They're so big!"

Joel rested his chin on the edge of the display of peaches. They were in a large bin. He was grinning, and his eyes were wide with delight as he stared at the piles of ripe, reddish-orange fruit. His father came up behind him.

"You know I can't buy any, Joel. I only have enough for the milk."

He held up the milk bottle and bent down to speak close to Joel's ear, his voice soft and sad. He was always sad when he spoke of money. They had so little. Papa worked very hard, but he didn't get paid very much. Mama couldn't work because Grandma was ill, and she had to care for her. Since Grandma came, there was no money for anything extra.

Joel frowned and blinked his eyes. As he turned to his father, he changed his face to a grin so he looked very happy. He didn't want Papa to feel bad.

"That's okay," he said as he took Papa's hand and turned away from the display. "I just wanted you to see them. They're so pretty."

Papa smiled and led the way to the exit. Joel walked, looking back to see the peaches until they were out of sight.

"Papa?"

Papa stopped on the sidewalk and looked down at Joel.

"Know what? Someday I'm going to have lots of money, and I'm going to go in the store and buy three peaches."

He held up three fingers, and his eyes sparkled. "Three peaches!"

"And I'm going to stand right here and eat one. Right away!"

He pretends to gobble up a peach. "I won't even wait until I get home. And I'll put the other two in my pockets and take them home and put them in my drawer. And I'll open the drawer before I go to bed and look at them. I won't eat them. I'll just look at them. And then I'll go to bed. And when I wake up…"

He looked up, and Papa smiled, caught up in Joel's dream.

"What will you do then?" he asked.

Joel sighed.

"I'll eat one for breakfast," he said softly, closing his eyes to see it, and he laughed.

Papa laughed with him. "What about the other peach?"

"I'll save it all day and all night and when I wake up…"

"You'll eat it!" Papa laughed. "And won't that be good?"

"Yes! Yes!" Joel shouted joyously, dancing all around Papa, his whole body wiggling with delight.

Papa hugged him, and they both smiled at such a wonderful dream.

Then Papa stood up and said, "We'd better get home. Mama will have our supper waiting."

Joel nodded, and they started walking again, each lost in his own thoughts. Suddenly, Joel stopped, his face serious. "Papa," he said slowly, "do you think I will ever buy three peaches—all at once—just for me?"

Papa looked down at him. He thought for a moment then nodded his head and said, "You will, Joel. Someday you will. I'm sure of it."

Joel nodded and grinned and skipped happily the rest of the way home.

The next day as he walked to school, he told his friends Paul and Mikey about his pretend peaches. They all laughed. They couldn't buy peaches either. It was a poor neighborhood, and there wasn't any extra money. Peaches were just a nice dream.

Then, suddenly Paul said in a very excited voice, "We should do that!"

The other two boys looked at him puzzled.

"What?" asked Mikey.

"Help Joel get his three peaches! And three for you. And three for me."

"How?" Joel asked.

"From the store! Mr. Gerry's store!"

"But we don't have any money," Mikey said. "He doesn't give them away, you know!"

"Yeah," Joel laughed. "I wish he did. I'd grab as many as I could carry!"

Paul laughed, too.

"That's what we'll do!" Paul was almost shouting with excitement. "We'll take them! We'll just take them!"

Joel and Mikey stared at him, then at each other, both frowning.

Mikey said softly, "You mean—you mean steal them?" His voice dropped to a whisper, and he looked around to be sure no one heard. No one was looking at them.

Paul whispered now, too. "Yes!"

Mikey said, "You mean really steal them? But how?"

"Wait!" Joel interrupted. "We can't do that. We would be in big trouble. Stealing is bad. My dad said so. We could go to jail!"

Paul laughed again. "You're such a baby! They don't put little kids like us in jail. The worst that would happen if we got caught, we'd be grounded. But we won't get caught. Cuz I have a plan!"

Paul spoke very softly now, and the boys had to lean in to hear him. *A plan?* they thought. They listened very carefully to Paul, then they looked at each other. A plan! It sounded like a good plan. It sounded like it could work! All three were grinning and high-fiving when the school bell rang.

After school, the three boys started walking home, but today was different. They didn't go home. Instead, they turned off at Center Street, and in a few minutes, they were standing in front of Mr. Gerry's store. All three were nervous. Joel hung back. He had been thinking about this all day. Now, it was actually going to happen. He knew Papa would be ashamed of him if he found out. He didn't want Papa to be ashamed of him. But he couldn't see any way out. He told them he would do it. He couldn't back out now. He gulped and stepped forward to stand with them.

"Remember the plan," Paul whispered. "Are you ready?'

The three did a high five, and Paul went into the store.

Mikey and Joel stood at the corner of the big front window and watched Paul in the store. The big display of peaches was right by the front door where you saw it as you walked in.

They could see Paul taking to Mr. Gerry, then Mr. Gerry pointed towards the back of the store. Paul said something, and Mr. Gerry nodded and started towards the back of the store with Paul right behind him. Paul pretended to scratch the top of his head. That was the signal. Mikey and Joel entered the store, crouching slightly, hoping no one would notice them. There was no one by the peaches.

Each boy put three peaches in a plastic produce bag and then Mikey added two more and Joel added one. Now they had nine, three for each of them. They set the bags on the edge of the display and carefully looked around. No one was near; no one was watching. They looked at each other and nodded, then abruptly grabbed the produce bags, stuffed them under their t-shirts and hurried out of the store, trying to look like just another customer. They started walking towards the corner but got scared and then they were running, clutching the bags. As soon as they turned the corner, they stopped, panting and peeked around the corner of the building. No one had followed them. They caught their breath and finally calmed down, and when they peeked again, Paul was walking slowly down the street. When he came around the corner, all three boys started jumping up and down with excitement.

"We did it!" Mikey shouted.

Paul grabbed his arm and said, "Shush!"

Mikey nodded.

Paul peeked around the corner again, then smiled and signaled for them to follow him. They hurried down the block to the nearby park, and all three sat on a bench under a tree facing away from the playground equipment. They looked around to be sure no one was watching them, Satisfied they were safe, Mikey and Joel brought the produce bags out from under their t-shirts and opened the bags.

The three boys stared into the bags at the ripe, luscious peaches for a moment, grinning, then set Mikey's bag on the bench. Mikey and Paul each grabbed a peach and started munching, grinning and laughing in between bites. They looked at Joel and stopped.

"What's wrong, Joel" Paul asked. Mikey took another bite and watched.

Joel was holding a peach, but he wasn't biting it. He was just staring at it. He did not look happy.

"What's wrong, Joel?" Paul repeated.

Joel looked up at them, then he stood up. He reached into his bag and took out a peach and handed it to Paul.

"This one is yours," he said. Paul accepted the peach.

"Aren't you going to eat yours?" Paul asked.

"No," he said. "I'm going to take them home. I just remembered my dad gets home early today. I have to hide the peaches before he gets home."

He turned away and started walking.

"Bye, guys," he said over his shoulder. "See you tomorrow."

"Remember, you can't tell anybody about this," Paul called after him.

"I know," Joel answered. He could hear Mikey and Paul laughing behind him. His stomach hurt.

Joel usually went in the front door and called to Mama and went to the kitchen and kissed her cheek before he went to his bedroom. But today, when he got home, he went in the back door because it was closer to his bedroom. He opened the door carefully so he could sneak in without Mama knowing. His heart was pounding, and his stomach hurt. His throat had a big lump in it, and that hurt too. The bag of peaches seemed very heavy.

He went into his room and closed the door. Then, he opened the drawer in the dresser and put the peaches in there, one by one, in the back of the drawer. He stared at them for a long time. They smell really good, he thought. Then he closed the drawer.

He lay down on his bed and stared at the ceiling. His stomach still hurt. He wondered if it would hurt forever.

After a while, Mama opened the door carrying a pile of his clothes that she had just washed. She was surprised to see him.

"I didn't hear you come in," she said. When he did not answer, she frowned. She set the clothes on his dresser and came over to the bed. She leaned down and felt his forehead.

"No fever," she said as she sat down on the edge of the bed. "Are you all right? Are you sick?"

Joel gulped to keep from crying. Mama was so nice, and he was—a thief! If she knew what he did, she would never like him again.

"I don't feel good," he said softly. "My stomach hurts."

"Maybe you ate something bad?"

Joel nodded. *I didn't eat it*, he thought, *but…*

Mama kissed his cheek. "Rest a bit."

She stood up and walked to the door. "I'll come get you for dinner."

Joel stuffed his hand in his mouth to keep from telling her how bad he was. When the door was closed, he got up and opened the drawer and looked at the peaches. Tears streamed down his cheeks. He sniffed his nose and wiped the tears with his sleeve. He went back to bed and tried to sleep, but he couldn't sleep. He kept thinking of the peaches, and then he would get up and open the drawer. A thief. He was a thief!

He heard Papa come home and then he heard Papa hurrying down the hallway. Joel lay very still pretending to be asleep.

"Joel?" Papa called softly when he opened the door. Joel pretended not to hear and didn't move. Papa came to the bed. Joel could hear him praying. He knew Papa would be holding his hands spread apart over Joel as he prayed. Then, he kissed Joel's cheek and went out, closing the door softly behind him.

When Papa came back to get him for dinner, Joel was standing by the dresser peering into the drawer.

When Papa opened the door, Joel quickly closed the drawer and moved back to the bed. He sat down on the edge of the bed and looked up at Papa.

"I don't feel good," he said. "I don't want any dinner. I'm just going to sleep."

Papa nodded.

Joel lay down, and Papa pulled up the covers for him and brushed Joel's hair back from his face. Joel closed his eyes. Papa smiled at him and kissed his cheek and left the room.

Joel was restless all night, sleeping off and on, having bad dreams of being chased and someone calling him a thief and a voice kept saying "make it right" and "do the right thing." He kept waking up, and each time he did, he checked the drawer. He hoped the peaches would disappear, and it would all be just a bad dream. But they were still there, and he was still a thief.

In the morning when Mama came to his room to see if he was better, he said he was.

"You look tired," she said. "Are sure you want to go to school?"

He said he did, and Mama said "Okay, but you must eat something first. You had no dinner."

He agreed, and she went back to the kitchen to make him scrambled eggs, his favorite.

As soon as he was alone, he dressed and put the peaches back in the produce bag and put the bag under his shirt. Then he went down the hall and opened the back door. He set the bag on top the garbage can and went in for breakfast.

He left the house for school through the front door as always. Then, so Mama wouldn't see him through the windows, he bent over and crept around to the back of the house and got the produce bag and put it under his shirt and started walking to school. He hoped he was late and wouldn't meet Mikey and Paul. But there they were at the corner waiting for him.

They were talking and laughing and waved at Joel. He caught up to them and said, "I'm not going to school."

"Why not?" asked Mikey.

Joel took a deep breath and spoke very fast. "I'm going to Mr. Gerry and tell him what I did and give him back the peaches."

The other two boys were stunned.

Paul grabbed Joel's shoulder and waved his fist in Joel's face.

"You better not tell him about us!"

Joel tried to pull away from Paul, but Paul was holding on very tight. The produce bag was hanging down below Joel's shirt, and Mikey grabbed for it. He caught the corner of the bag and pulled. The bag flew out from under Joel's shirt and hit the ground. Mikey grabbed it up and opened it.

"All three peaches are still here. You didn't eat any!" Mikey held up the bag so Paul could see inside. Paul turned to look in the bag and loosened his grip on Joel's shirt.

"Give me that bag!" Joel yelled, jerking it away from Paul. He shoved Paul and Paul fell down. Joel grabbed the bag and started running. Paul and Mikey followed. They caught Joel at the corner of the block, and both grabbed at him. Mikey caught his shirt and knocked Joel down. Paul grabbed the bag and fell, and the peaches flew out of the bag and landed, rolling in the grass. Joel and Paul both scrambled after the peaches. Paul grabbed one peach, and Mikey grabbed one, and they ran down the street. Paul stopped and looked back at Joel who was slowly picking up the last peach, its' skin hanging off on one side.

As Joel held it up sadly, Paul yelled, "You better not tell! You'd better not tell!"

Then Mikey and Paul ran down the block toward school laughing.

Joel gulped and wiped his eyes. Nothing was going right. This was the worst two days of his life.

He was really sorry for what he did, but nobody would care. He stole the peaches. He should have never done that. Then he didn't tell Mama and Papa. That was just like telling a lie. He shouldn't have done that either. And now his friends didn't like him anymore, and he couldn't even take the peaches back because two of them were gone. And this one…

He held up the peach with its torn skin hanging down. He touched the flap of skin, and it flopped back and forth. He blinked his eyes, then he picked up the produce bag and put the peach in it. Then he walked over to the bus stop bench and sat down.

What now?

He thought for a long time, just sitting there.

He could go back home and tell Mama he was sick, another lie, and hide in his bedroom. But he would have to come out sometime and then he would have to tell Mama and Papa why he was hiding in his room. And they would say, "Do the right thing." That made him remember his dream, and his stomach started to hurt again.

Maybe he would just stay here on the bench. But, no, after a while somebody would make him get up.

What could he do? What should he do?

When he left the house, he was going to go see Mr. Gerry. He thought about that for a while. Then he stood up and picked up the produce bag. He didn't try to hide it under his shirt. He looked back toward his house. Then he looked toward his school. Then he turned and started down the block to Mr. Gerry's store.

He stopped in front of the store and peered through the window. Mr. Gerry was putting carrots in a display bin. He was very careful and lined the carrots up so they all looked very nice. Joel bit his lip, took a big breath, gulped once, then turned and pushed the store door open and walked in. Mr. Gerry heard the door open and turned.

Joel stopped just inside and looked at Mr. Gerry. Mr. Gerry looked at Joel and smiled.

"Well, young man, what can I do for you today?"

Joel took another big breath, then marched over to Mr. Gerry with his head down and handed him the produce bag.

"I—I tried to… I mean I wanted to—I mean…"

He looked up and saw Mr. Gerry looking into the bag with a puzzled look on his face.

"My goodness, this peach looks terrible. I can't believe you bought this at my store. Please replace it with my apologies." He looked up at Joel who now was sobbing.

Mr. Gerry put his arm around Joel's shoulder and patted his back.

"Well, young man, I guess you'd better tell me what this is all about."

Joel nodded then spoke very fast. "I stole it, sir. I'm a thief. I knew it was a bad thing to do, but we did it anyway. I'm really sorry. I didn't eat any. I was bringing them back, but then they got wrecked, and this is the only one I could save. And it's broken."

Joel's head was down. He couldn't see Mr. Gerry smile and shake his head.

"Well, young man, you're right. You did a very bad thing. Can you tell me who else was with you?"

"No, sir," Joel mumbled, "I can't."

Joel looked up. Mr. Gerry was looking up at the ceiling, thinking. Joel's legs wanted to run away, but he wouldn't let them.

"Well, young man, I think the best thing to do here is for you to pay for the peaches. If you do that, I don't think I have to call the police. What do you say to that?"

"I can't pay for them cuz I got no money. I guess you better call the police now."

"No money, huh? Hmmm." Mr. Gerry thought for a moment, scratching his chin looking at the broken peach. "Well, are you willing to work? You could do some work for me, and I would pay you, and then you could pay for the peaches. What do you say to that?"

"Oh, yes sir!" Joel stood up as straight and tall as he could. "I'm really strong, and my dad says I'm smart and—I'll do any work you want, sir. Thank you, sir. Thank you."

Mr. Gerry held back the smile that wanted to come out and said as seriously as he could because this was a very serious thing, "Well, young man, I need some help putting some cans and bottles on the shelves—and some sweeping is needed in the back room—and some cereal needs unpacking—oh, and those candy packages in back were supposed to come out yesterday."

He looked at Joel and said slowly, "I'm going to give you a second chance, young man. I hope you won't let me down."

"I won't let you down, sir. Thank you."

"Well, come on then. I'll show you where the stock is and where it should go in the store."

Mr. Gerry took Joel back to the stockroom and showed him where everything was. He told him he could not climb the ladder because you had to have special training for that. Without special training, he could only do the stock that was down on the bottom storage shelf. Then, they went back into the store, and Mr. Gerry showed Joel where the stock would go. He said if Joel couldn't reach the shelf in the store, he should call Mr. Gerry and he would help him use the two-step ladder. Then, Joel went back to the stock room and started working. Mr. Gerry took the peach and went into his office for a few minutes. When he came out, he was smiling. Then he went back to arranging the carrots.

Mr. Gerry showed Joel how to use the little push cart. Joel took the cans and cereal boxes and soap out of the packing boxes and put them on the little cart. The cart had three shelves. Each shelf had a ridge around it so things didn't fall off. He filled all three shelves, then pushed it into the store and put the things on the store shelves. Joel worked very hard.

Mr. Gerry gave him a sandwich from the deli counter for lunch. Joel was very hungry. After lunch, he suggested Joel take a nap. After all, he wasn't used to working this hard. Joel was tired. He was glad to lay down in the stock room on a cot in the corner. He slept a long time. When he woke, he started working again. He knew what to do. About two o'clock, Mr. Gerry said Joel had worked long enough. He was actually surprised at how much Joel had gotten done.

He gave Joel three dollars. Joel stared at the money in his hand for a long time. It was a lot of money.

"Mr. Gerry, he asked, "How much is it for nine peaches?"

"I thought you only took three peaches."

"I need to pay for nine peaches, sir."

"Well," Mr. Gerry replied. "It depends on how much they weigh." "How heavy they are," he added when Joel looked puzzled.

Joel put nine peaches into the hanging produce scale. They waited a moment for it to stop swinging. Then, Mr. Gerry said, "Three dollars and twenty-seven cents."

Joel was dismayed; he didn't have that much. He held up the three dollar bills.

Mr. Gerry looked at them and said, "I'm sorry; I made a mistake. I must have counted wrong. You should have four dollars."

He opened the cash register and took out another dollar and handed it to Joel.

"Is there anything else you want to buy?"

"No, sir," Joel replied, "Just the peaches."

Mr. Gerry rang up the sale, and Joel gave him the four dollars. When Mr. Gerry held out the change, Joel shook his head no and wouldn't take it.

"You take it, son." Mr. Gerry smiled as he dropped the coins in Joel's pants pocket. "You worked hard and earned it. And now, I guess it's time for you to go home."

Joel nodded. "Thank you, sir," he said turning to the door.

"Wait," Mr. Gerry called. Joel turned back.

Mr. Gerry was holding out the bag of peaches. "You forgot your peaches. You paid for them."

"No, thank you, sir. I can't take them. I paid for peaches that were stole. I can't keep something that I stole." And Joel went out the door to home.

When Joel got home, he knew he had to tell Mama and Papa what he had done. He went into the kitchen and kissed Mama's check. Then he sat down at the table and said, "I have to tell you something when Papa gets home."

"Okay," she said. "Are you hungry? I made peanut butter cookies, your favorite." She held up a cookie.

"No, thank you," he replied solemnly and went down the hall to his room. Mama watched him go, his head down, shoulders slumped. *He's so sad*, she thought.

Joel lay on his bed staring at the ceiling. He didn't want to tell them, but he knew he had too. His stomach hurt from trying not to cry. After a bit, he fell asleep. He dreamed about peaches. They were chasing him, and they had teeth and threatened to eat him. They yelled and threw things at him.

He cried out just as Papa came into his room. Papa shook him and woke him up. When Joel looked up, he saw Papa and threw his arms around Papa's neck and cried and cried. Mama patted his back and whispered, "It's okay. It will be all right, Joel."

Finally, he calmed down. He sat on the edge of the bed, and Papa and Mama sat beside him, waiting. It was very hard to tell them, but he did it. He told them everything he had done. He did not tell them about

Paul and Mikey. When he finished, he gave Mama the change from the store and the receipt for the peaches.

Mama said she was proud of him for making it right. She wiped tears from her eyes and hugged him and kissed his forehead. Then she had to run to the kitchen when the food timer started dinging loudly.

"I am proud of you, too," Papa said. "You did a bad thing, but then you were sorry and you made it right. That makes me proud of you. I love you, son."

Joel was so relieved. "I love you, too, Papa."

"Joel, I know you didn't do the stealing by yourself. Who was with you?"

"I promised, Papa. I can't say."

"Okay. When I stopped at the store on the way home tonight, I saw Mikey and Paul talking to Mr. Gerry. The boys were crying. Their parents were with them. I heard Mr. Gerry say all it takes for people to do the right thing is for someone to do it first. I think he was talking about you. Now, come, dinner is ready."

That night, Joel slept well, no bad dreams. In the morning, he checked the drawer, no peaches. He smiled.

When Joel started walking to school the next day, he saw Paul and Mikey waiting for him at the corner. He wondered what they would do.

"I never told on you," he said as he cautiously approached them.

"Yeah," Paul said, "we know."

Mikey blurted out, "Did you know Mr. Gerry has cameras in the store taking pictures of customers? He showed us the pictures of us stealing the peaches."

"Yeah," Paul added, "He called our parents and told them what we did. My dad said he was disappointed in me." Paul's face scrunched as he gulped so he wouldn't cry. He continued in a sad, small voice, his lip quivering, "I wished he was mad at me instead."

"Yeah. My mom cried. I don't want to make my mom cry," Mikey sniffed.

"Yeah," Joel agreed, "Me, too."

They were quiet then, each one thinking, wishing they could take back what they had done.

Paul said, "Now we're grounded because we didn't 'fess up before Mr. Gerry called."

"Maybe forever!" Mikey added.

"Me, too," said Joel.

Mikey grimaced. "I heard he made you work all day to pay for the peaches. We have to work ,too."

"Yeah," Paul shook his head. "On Saturday, we have to be there at 9:00 in the morning until noon to pay for the peaches we took."

Mikey added, "We each have to pay for all nine peaches. That doesn't seem fair. Did you have to pay for all nine?"

Joel started to laugh.

"What are you laughing about?

"Nothing, really. I'm just so glad I didn't have to go to jail. I'll never steal anything ever again. It gave me the worst stomachache." He looked at his two best friends. "It even made us mad at each other. We almost stopped being friends. We are still friends, aren't we?"

"Sure," Mikey said.

"Of course," Paul added.

"Great," Joel grinned. "Oh, I did have to pay for all nine peaches, too."

"I guess we better get going or we'll be late for school." Mikey started walking, and the others joined him.

"I wonder how long we'll be grounded."

"Do you think they'll let us talk on the phone, at least?"

"I don't know. Hey," Joel laughed. "I'll come on Saturday and wave at you while you're working, okay?"

"Okay."

"Great."

"My brother Johnny says there's a law so people can't make kids work, but my dad said I have to work for Mr. Gerry anyway."

"Yeah, my dad says that law doesn't count if you're a thief."

"Oh, that's why."

"So, Joel, when you get big, are you still going to buy three peaches all at once?"

"Yeah, I am."

"Me, too."

"Me, too."

"Race you to the corner!"

"I'll beat you!"

"Losers are peaches!"

"I'm no peach!"

"Me, neither!"

"Peaches!" they all shouted as they ran down the sidewalk.

Three months later, on Joel's birthday, Papa gave him a produce bag with three peaches in it. Papa laughed. "Eat one now," he said. "And one tomorrow and one the next day. Right, Joel?"

Joel picked up one of the peaches. He stared at it for a long time. Then he looked in the bag and shook his head. He put the peach back in the bag.

"I'm sorry, Joel." Papa was perplexed. "We thought you'd like the peaches."

Joel looked up.

"I like the peaches, Papa but…"

Joel thought a moment.

"I'm not going to eat them all, just me." He grinned.

"I'm going to give one to Mama." He handed a peach to her.

"And one to you, Papa." He gave a peach to Papa.

Then he took out the last peach. "And one to me."

He held up the peach and laughed. "We can go to the park and sit on a bench, all of us, and eat the peaches, all of us, all at once."

They all smiled.

"And when I'm big, that's what I'm gonna do then, too. I'll buy three peaches all at once and get two friends to eat them with me."

Joel lifted the peach to his face and inhaled the sweet aroma.

"Ummm, peaches," Joel said, and they all laughed.

WHEN CADIE WAS BORN

When Cadie was born, her bottom started coming out first. The doctor pushed her back in, then realized the umbilical cord was around her neck. It took a while to turn her and release her from the cord. She came out head first, but her face was blue, and she didn't make a sound. The doctor turned her upside down and slapped her bottom. She still didn't cry. He was suctioning her mouth when her mother started screaming, "Breathe, Cadie, breathe!" And Cadie did. She threw her head back, took a sputtering breath, and howled. Her face turned red, and she howled some more. Everyone breathed a sigh of relief.

Cadie went home on the tenth of December wrapped in a heavy blanket and covered with love. The Minnesota sky was gray, and snow fell softly. Diane and Peter held her and fed her and kissed her and loved her. This was their first child, and they smiled happily and looked forward to her crawling and running and climbing. Diane noticed that Cadie threw her arms but didn't move her legs but thought she must be tired.

When she didn't move them the next day either, she called the clinic. Come right in, they said.

After checking Cadie, the doctor looked sad. "The lack of oxygen at birth," she said. "Cadie might never move. She might stay just as she is, forever."

"But is her brain okay? Can she think?" The doctor hesitated then shook her head. "I can't tell."

They went home, and Peter listened, ashen-faced, to the doctor's report. Then, they hugged Cadie between them and wept long, hard sobs until they ran out of tears. They promised each other they would care for her always and love her and be there for her and for each other. The day before Christmas, Peter left. He wrote a goodbye note; it was too hard, he couldn't do it, and they would be better off without him anyway. They never saw him again.

Diane cried that night for a long time. Then she got up and put the wedding pictures and silver goblets in a box and put it in the storage area in the basement. She looked at her daughter sleeping peacefully, kissed her good night, and went to bed. She said goodbye to what might have been and accepted what was.

The next morning, Diane fed Cadie, then stretched her arms and legs and rolled her from side-to-side and over and over. Diane laid on the floor on her back and put Cadie on her tummy and looked at her and talked to her. "I'm here, Cadie. Look at me, Cadie. Lift your head, Cadie." Cadie didn't respond, but her eyes looked into Diane's eyes, and Diane was sure they were connecting. Cadie knew her mother. Cadie knew her mother loved her. And that was enough.

Every day, Diane did the same routine. Breakfast, stretching and rolling, then shopping for the day's food and looking for toys that Cadie might like. They went to the library, and Diane read every book she could find on how to bring movement back to a frozen little body. They stopped to look at everything. Diane pointed out the flowers, the trees, the neighbor's dog, then the neighbors and the people in the shops, and most of all, the snow. Cadie stared at anything that was right in front of her. The snow, though, made her smile when it landed on her cheeks. After a while, everyone knew who Cadie was and wondered how her mom could be so cheery when things were so hard for her. And always, Diane hugged Cadie and kissed her and told her how wonderful and beautiful and smart she was.

And Cadie listened. She couldn't speak, but she started understanding what her mother said. It was like coming out of a coma. The day Cadie lifted her head for the first time, Diane ran outside with Cadie and shouted for joy. She ran to the neighbors and the shops and told the dog next door. Cadie moved!

Time passed. Diane never looked back. She never dated. She worked at home on the computer doing bookkeeping and telemarketing for a small automotive accessories company. Cadie was her world.

Very slowly, Cadie progressed. They couldn't get her legs to work, but her upper body started taking orders from her brain. Her muscles were weak but getting stronger all the time. By the time she was six, she could use her right hand to move her electric wheelchair by pushing the power button. She could speak but not very clearly. But Diane could understand. She could draw and color and even use the scissors. Cadie worked very hard, and so did Diane. Cadie was in school now in a special class and loved it

Winter was always special for them. The snow never ceased to make Cadie smile. As she grew, they played in the snow together, built snowmen, and made snow angels by lying in the snow and moving their arms. Cadie smiled and laughed out loud and was a happy little girl. For Diane, it was enough.

Every year, Diane took two weeks of vacation in the summer. She and Cadie lounged and went to the parks and the zoo and enjoyed every moment. This year, their vacation started on a Friday in June, two weeks after school ended. Cadie was six and a half.

That Sunday, Diane's folks had a BBQ for some friends. George and Joni Benson came with their son, David, who was visiting from Tucson. When he met Diane, she sat and talked with him, just to be polite. He was a programmer for a handmade tiles manufacturer. He didn't brag. He just seemed—nice. David told her she had a smile like sunshine. He stared at her so much it embarrassed her. He was charming and attentive and never left her side.

The next day, he called her. Would she have lunch with him? She hesitated then said yes. It didn't mean anything. But he was with her almost constantly after that. Sometimes, Cadie came with them, but often it was just the two of them. They talked and laughed and enjoyed each other's company. Cadie seemed to like him. The more Diane looked at him, the more handsome he seemed. Then he kissed her, and she started dreading the day he would leave. And it scared her.

They were at the zoo with Cadie looking at the Komodo dragon when he proposed. Diane was surprised and excited and afraid. She didn't know what to say. Deep inside, she felt a pain and wondered if she dared trust him. He seemed comfortable with Cadie. But get married? What would Cadie think?

David turned around and asked her. "Cadie, what would you say if your mom and I got married? Would you be okay with that?"

Cadie looked at David then at Diane. She frowned for a moment then smiled.

David said solemnly, "I was thinking you might want to be my best man."

Cadie started laughing uproariously.

Diane went to Cadie and lifted her chin and smiled. "I would love for you to be my maid of honor," she said softly.

She felt David's arms envelope both her and Cadie.

"Does that mean you'll marry me?" he whispered.

"Yes," she and Cadie answered at the same time. They all laughed.

Two weeks. They had known each other only two weeks. Diane still couldn't believe he had asked her to marry him two weeks after he met her, and even stranger, that she had said yes. She was quiet, steady, not impulsive at all, and very distrusting of men—and yet she had said yes. David helped her pack her personal things, and she made the wedding arrangements. A week later, Diane married David in the heat of summer in Minnesota in the small church in which her mother and grandmother were married. Cadie was the maid of honor, and David's father was his best man. They became a family.

And then they moved from hot, humid Minnesota to hotter, dry Arizona. Diane shipped some things but chose to leave all her furniture and dishes and towels and linens. David assured her she could change colors or replace everything in his—correction, their—house if she wanted. "It's our house now."

It was a grand adventure. It was hectic, crazy, exhausting, and chaotic. It was heaven.

David had a one-story house on the edge of Tucson. They were surrounded on three sides by other small houses. From their large back window, they had a breathtaking view of the open desert. Many of their neighbors were retired people with free time during the day, and they welcomed Diane and Cadie. Marian and Barney lived across the street. Their door was always open, and Marian dropped off dinners while they were moving in and offered to have Cadie come over to visit or go along to the Ice Cream Shack. The new family went to BBQs and drove all over looking at the desert and the small towns. They even drove down to the Mexican border towns.

Diane found a job doing bookkeeping for a small company. They let her work mostly from home. Diane and David were kindred spirits and rarely disagreed. When school started, Cadie made a few friends who didn't seem to care that she was in a chair and had trouble speaking. Nice kids, they included and pro-tected Cadie at school. She hadn't yet made friends to play with after school. She never complained, but Diane could see she was lonely.

They all looked forward to going "home" for Christmas. The weather here was nice, but they had grown up with snow at Christmas. Snowball fights, making snow angels, seeing all the relatives, singing Christmas carols for the neighbors standing in the snow, all bundled up, cheeks red. Life was good. It was enough.

But then, in November, David got laid off. The company was really sorry and hoped to rehire him in the spring, but they had lost two large accounts and ...

David looked for another job, but no one was hiring. "Try again after the holidays" was the answer he kept getting. He finally got hired as a waiter at a local restaurant, Jackson's Oasis. He planned to work there only until they went north for the holidays. He laughed self-consciously when he told Diane. Cadie, though, was thrilled and laughed happily as he showed them his uniform: black slacks, white shirt, and black tie. It reminded her of the wedding. Money was tight, but they would be okay now, and he was sure something would turn up in January. Diane's mom sent money for the tickets. Soon they would be in Minnesota with loved ones for two whole weeks for Christmas. And there would be snow there. It would be great!

Except they couldn't go.

Cadie woke them in the middle of the night, coughing violently. She had a fever and was shaking. When she started throwing up, they rushed her to the hospital. The emergency room doctor wasn't sure what was wrong but decided it was too risky to send her home. She was admitted, put on an IV, and given antibiotics. Diane and David stayed in the room with her dozing in chairs by her bed. She threw up several more times during the night, each time falling back exhausted against the pillow. In the morning, they ran a battery of tests. She had contracted some kind of stomach bug. Cadie couldn't throw it off. And now her breathing became labored. Cadie had been through several difficult hospitalizations before. She did her best to rally, and Diane helped her. Smiling and making light of things had gotten them through before and would again.

David, though, was terrified. Cadie suddenly frightened him. He didn't know what to say or do to make things better. When Cadie was released from the hospital, the doctor was adamant that she could not travel for several months, especially north.

They couldn't go home to Minnesota. Diane sent the check back and cried with her mom on the phone. Then they all prepared for their first Christmas in Arizona.

Diane unpacked her small box of Christmas decorations. She had kept only those few ornaments that really meant something to her and Cadie. David had nothing. He had never decorated because he always went north. None of them had expected to be in Arizona on Christmas. Cadie understood that she wouldn't see her grandparents, but somehow she still expected it to snow. She was surprised and disappointed when they told her it didn't snow in Tucson.

The night before Christmas Eve, when David and Diane were in the kitchen together before he went to work, he said in a frustrated voice, "Everything is so expensive for Cadie. My insurance doesn't cover as much as yours did. And now, paying the whole premium myself, it's so much money. Things just aren't going the way I wanted. What kind of a Christmas is this anyway? I can't even afford to buy presents. I wanted everything to be perfect for us, but everything is so hard. I feel so helpless. I miss the whole Christmas thing with my folks, the get-togethers, the caroling. I even miss the snow. How goofy is that, to miss the snow?" He was quiet for a moment. "This is the first year I won't be home for Christmas with my family."

Diane caught her breathe when he said that. *But we* are *home*, she thought. *This is our home. We are your family.*

Cadie overheard him as she was coming down the hall. She stopped for a moment, her eyes wide, then turned her chair abruptly and returned to her room.

After David left for work, Cadie came out to the kitchen where Diane sat at the table, her head down.

"Mom, I don't think David likes me anymore."

Diane was startled. "What?"

"He can't go home for Christmas now because of me, and he loves the snow, and there's no snow here. And he misses his family. And I cost too much money." She paused, then looked down and spoke in a wavering voice, "If I wasn't here, he could go back home. You both could."

She turned her chair suddenly and went down the hall to her room and closed the door.

Diane was so stunned she didn't react right away. Then she jumped up and ran to Cadie's room. She knocked on the door. They had a rule about never entering a bedroom unless you were invited. Bedrooms were private. "Cadie, may I come in?" She thought she heard muffled crying.

Cadie's voice came softly through the door. "No, mom. I'm going to sleep now. I'm tired."

Diane stood outside the door for a moment then reluctantly went back to the kitchen. She would talk to David when he got home, and together they would convince Cadie that he did love her, and everything would be all right. Suddenly, Diane felt that stab of pain, the same one she had when Peter left. David had sounded so frustrated. Could Cadie be right? Was his life too hard now? *Oh, Lord, please don't let him walk away like Peter did. Please.*

She waited up for David. When he was more than an hour late, she called the restaurant. There was no answer. After another hour, she considered calling the police. She decided to wait. When she heard the key in the lock, she realized she had fallen asleep on the couch. She sat up just as he came into the living room. His eyes were red from crying. He sat down next to her and gently put his arms around her. "I'm so sorry," he said. "I just had to think. I love you. I love Cadie. We'll be okay. We just need to stick together." Diane smiled and relaxed. They talked for a long time then went to bed. They would talk to Cadie in the morning.

At breakfast, they waited in vain for Cadie. She would always call when she was ready to get up, and Diane would go in and help her. When she didn't call, Diane decided to wake her. She knocked on the door. There was no answer. She knocked again. No answer. Diane decided to break the "do not enter without permission" rule. She opened the door slowly.

"Cadie?" she called. Silence. She opened the door wide and looked in. The wheelchair wasn't next to the bed. She stepped into the room and looked around. The bed was empty. Cadie wasn't there! As she stood staring at the bed, she noticed a folded paper on the floor. "Mom" was scrawled on it. She picked it up and unfolded it. There were only a few words. Cadie was learning to write but not very well yet. Diane could barely make out the words. She stared at it then took a deep breath. 'i go yu be hapy cadie'.

"David!" she called. "Cadie's not here!"

David heard her and ran to Cadie's room. She held out the note. David read it, puzzled at first then shocked as he realized. She had run away! Diane told him what Cadie had said the night before.

Her wheelchair was gone. They searched the whole house and even the garage.

"She's gone, David. She left the house!"

"She left the house? But—but how? Someone would have to help her into her chair."

"Oh, David. Since we got here, she's been working on her upper body strength so she could lift herself from the bed to the chair. She's done it a couple of times. She worked so hard. We were going to get a folding chair for her so she could ride in your car sometimes in one of the passenger seats." She paused, "She was going to surprise you."

David was dumbfounded. Cadie really was amazing. And now, she was gone because she thought he didn't want her. He closed his eyes for a moment, realizing his words were the reason Cadie left.

"But she's never left the house before," Diane continued.

Cadie had some friends at school but none near home. She knew the neighbors, but it was not likely she would go to one of the neighbors. They had paved streets, but the driveways were mostly gravel. There was a sidewalk but only on one side of the street. And there were curbs. Even a motorized wheelchair can't get up curbs.

Then another frightening thought occurred to Diane. She caught her breath.

"Oh, David, what if we don't find her?"

David shook his head. "I don't know," he said slowly.

He looked at Diane. When he saw the terror in her face, he quickly said, "No!"

He put his arms around Diane.

"I'm sure we'll find her," he added. "She must have gone somewhere."

"But where?!" Diane asked. "Where could she go? How could she?"

"I don't know." He thought a moment then said, "I'll take the car and look for her. You wait here in case she comes back."

At Diane's horrified look, he quickly added, "In case she comes back *before* I find her."

"I'll find her!" he repeated as he ran out the door.

Diane stood very still, her mind numb. Then she took a deep breath and forced herself to think about what she should do. *Call the police*, she thought. Should I call them right away or...? She thought back to the "Safety for living in the desert" book. A lady on the plane had given it to her. They had chatted, and she said she was part of the Welcome Wagon group. She said they wouldn't get out to Diane for probably several weeks, but Diane should have the book right away since she had a child. Diane had responded that Cadie never went anywhere alone, but the woman pointed to the sections on plants and other things to watch out for. Diane thanked her and read the entire book on the airplane. She didn't know there were so many things in the desert that could hurt you.

Could Cadie have gone into the desert? Alone? Diane didn't really think Cadie would do that but...

The book had also talked about volunteers who came at a moment's notice if a child was missing in the desert; the president of the bank, firefighters, school teachers, businessmen and women, teenagers—people from every walk of life. When a child was missing, they dropped everything and came, then joined hands and marched into the desert searching. If a child fell down, the book said, you couldn't see them when you looked out over the cactus and other plants. You had to walk it and look down, arm in arm. They even brought in helicopters! Call right away, the book said. A child could get dehydrated very quickly, and there were dangerous insects and snakes and animals. Even if you're not sure, call!

Diane ran to the kitchen and dialed 911.

Just as she hung up the phone, David came in the front door.

At Diane's questioning look, he responded, "I forgot my cell phone." He paused then said, "Diane, call 911. We have to find her quickly. They'll help."

Diane hugged David. "I already did. They're on their way."

"I'm going back out to look," David said, "There's open desert behind the house. I don't know if she's out there, but the chair has a motor so…"

Diane nodded. "I'll tell the sheriff."

She hugged him again, and he ran out the back door. She stood in the doorway and watched as he ran through their small yard into the desert. He stopped and looked around then started slowly walking back and forth from the far end of one neighbor's house to the far end of the other's.

Then she started calling everyone they knew. "We can't find Cadie. Have you seen here? Please look for her. Call me if you hear anything. Ask everyone you know to look for her." Diane's voice cracked, but she kept calling.

The sheriff arrived in less than ten minutes. A few minutes later, cars started pulling up out front, filling the street. The volunteers all ran to the front door, talked to the sheriff, then formed groups. Each group went a different way. Three of the groups went behind the house and joined David in his search. The open desert would be a very dangerous place for Cadie. Every man and woman who came was praying the same prayer. "Please let her be alive and okay. Help us find her quickly. Protect her."

They all knew that they were looking for a little girl in a wheelchair. In the desert, a wheelchair could easily overturn. She could be hurt. She was little. It would be hard to see her.

Diane was shaking with fear, but it gave her a tiny bit of comfort that they were so organized.

After a bit, David came back inside to get a drink.

"They have this area covered. I just wonder if she could have tried to get to the school. I'm going to drive over there. She can't get up a curb, but she could go down one."

He could see Diane was very close to hysteria. He hugged her.

"We'll find her. We. Will. Find. Her," he said in the most positive tone he could muster. "We will!"

He ran out the front door, and she heard the car start and leave. "We will," she repeated over and over. "We will, we will, we will."

David headed to the school almost a mile away. Cadie rode the special school bus. The bus picked up several students, and the route made a number of turns. If Cadie did come this way, she could have gotten lost. When he got to the school, the doors were locked. He searched the grounds but found nothing, and there was no one around to ask. David started driving slowly up and down the streets scanning the yards. At each corner, he stopped and stared down the cross street in both directions hoping to see her.

Whenever he saw children, he stopped and asked if they had seen a girl in a wheelchair. No luck.

Then he glanced in the rearview mirror and saw a small boy chasing his car and waving. David stopped and waited for the boy. The boy was about eight years old and took several minutes to catch his breath. He tried to talk but only got out a word or two at a time. David couldn't make out what he was saying. Finally, the boy spoke more normally.

"I saw her!" he shouted. "I saw her!"

"Where?" David's voice was excited, and he opened the door and jumped out. He reached for the boy, and the boy backed up. David pulled his hands back and held them up so the boy would not be afraid. David took a deep breath and forced himself to speak quietly and slowly. When he did, the boy relaxed and pointed back the way the way David had come.

David looked back. "Where did you see her? Could you show me?"

Again, the boy backed up. "No sir," he said, his voice was shaky with fear, and he swallowed.

David realized the boy was afraid to get in his car. He smiled and said, "Listen. Where is your house? You walk, and I will follow you. We will ask your mama if you can help me, okay?"

The boy nodded and started running down the street. David quickly got back in the car, did a U-turn, and followed the boy. When the boy ran up to one of the houses and went inside, David parked the car and followed. He knocked on the door, and a tall man opened it and scowled at David. "You tried to get my Jimmy in your car?" The man leaned forward, angry and threatening.

David backed up and said in a calm voice, "No sir, I didn't. My daughter is missing. I've been asking everybody if they've seen her. Jimmy said he saw my daughter in her wheelchair. I asked him to show me where. I was just going to follow him. I told him to go home and ask if he could help. I followed him in my car. Please," he pleaded. "He's the only person who's seen her. Cadie is little, just six. Please let him help me. You come, too. Please!"

The man stared at David for a moment then nodded and said, "I'll tell my wife."

David felt faint and leaned his arm against the door frame. The man and Jimmy were back in a moment. His wife stood in the doorway and said, "I see her on the TV, the little girl. I will pray for her. Now hurry!"

Jimmy's father held out his hand, and David shook it. "I am Miguel," he said.

"I'm David. Thank you, sir."

With Jimmy pointing the way, they drove to where he had seen Cadie. David stopped the car, and they all got out and searched the immediate area and looked in the backyards. They stared down the street in front of them. They could see open desert not far away.

They got back in the car and continued down the street. They stopped when the street ended. They sat in the car looking out at the endless expanse of desert all thinking the same thing: *If she is out there, where is she?*

They walked back and forth, searching, fifty feet wide and fifty feet into the desert. They found nothing. The brush wasn't broken, there were no wheelchair tracks.

Miguel shook his head and stopped searching. "She did not go into the desert here," he said.

David stood up and nodded. "I'll take you back." His voice broke as he said, "Where could she have gone?"

Miguel followed to the car. "We'll keep looking. We should check the yards again. Maybe she went through one of the yards."

Miguel and Jimmy walked up the sides of the street checking all the yards for anything.

David sat in the driver's seat for a moment staring out at the desert. He took out his cell and started to dial Diane then canceled the call. If the searchers had found anything, Diane would have called him. He didn't have any good news, so why call and make her more worried?

He started the car and drove up to the corner, then got out and walked back, checking yards as he went. Suddenly, he stopped. He squinted and stared hard across the yard. He could see what looked like a cleared space.

"Miguel!" he called, "Look at this!"

Miguel ran up to David and looked out where David was looking.

"What is that?" David asked.

Miguel stared then said excitedly, "It's Bucket Road! It goes across to a bunch of houses over there." He pointed left. This is the only road from there to the highway. It's just a dirt road, very old. Those are really old houses, run-down. It crosses a ravine before it gets to the houses."

David stared across the yard, a dirt road then desert. "A ravine? How deep is it?"

Miguel thought a moment. "I haven't been that way for years. I went once just to see it, but it's pretty bad. The ravine is probably twenty, twenty-five feet deep. I think it flash floods. Not now, though."

As they watched, a pack of dogs ran by through the desert toward the road. They started barking as they ran. It sounded menacing.

"Daddy, will the dogs hurt that girl?" Jimmy asked in a frightened voice.

Suddenly, David froze then ran back to the car. He yelled out the window as he passed them, "Get some boards or a rake or something to beat them off. And a gun if you have one!"

David roared down the street and into the desert. He prayed he wouldn't get stuck. He turned right sharply and headed for the dirt road. When he reached it, he made a sharp left turn onto the road. The tires squealed, and the car swerved, but he was able to straighten the car. He could see the pack of dogs running down the middle of the road. The barking grew louder. Suddenly, the pack stopped, and one of the dogs started circling back and forth. Then he heard a scream. Cadie!

He caught up to the dogs, and they scattered. He stopped the car and scanned the road ahead. Where was she?

He threw open the car door and jumped out. The dogs were standing back, but he knew they could attack any minute. The dogs were all different breeds, big, tiny and in-between, all scraggly and skinny. One by one, they had been dumped in the desert. Now they were a family. A large German Shepherd seemed to be the leader.

As David got closer to the dogs, he saw Cadie. She was screaming in terror. Her wheelchair had overturned and fallen into the ditch. Cadie was under the wheelchair, but her bare arms and her head were not covered. The dogs were between him and Cadie. The shepherd was pacing, waiting to see what David would do, getting ready to attack.

David knew that if the dogs attacked, he and Cadie would both be killed. He had nothing with which to defend themselves. He needed a weapon.

Slowly, David back stepped to the car. It was only a few feet but seemed like forever. "Don't attack," he prayed under his breath over and over. "Please, don't attack."

The car was still running, and the driver's door was still open. He paused when he reached the open door. The shepherd was watching him intently. Suddenly David jumped into the car and threw it into gear. The car lurched forward, and the dogs scattered. The shepherd backed off but didn't leave. The other dogs stopped and watched. And waited.

David stopped the car close to Cadie. The car was now between her and the dogs, but she wouldn't be safe until she was in the car with all the doors and windows closed. The shepherd could easily come through an open car window.

He still needed a weapon. He had a tire iron, but it was in the trunk. It would take too long to get it. He glanced into the back seat. Not much there, just what he picked up yesterday at the garden store: three potted plants for the front yard, a bag of fertilizer, pruning shears, and a shovel. And a flashlight! And he had just put in new batteries.

He jumped out, leaving the door open, and opened the back door. He grabbed one of the pots and heaved it over the car at the shepherd. It didn't hit the dog, but he backed up a few steps and stopped. David pulled out the pruning shears and shovel letting them fall to the ground. It spooked the shepherd, and he backed up a few more feet. He grabbed the flashlight, left the door open, and kicked the shovel and pruning shears into the ditch. Cadie had been screaming continuously. Now with David next to her, she stopped screaming and began crying, shaking with fear. He patted her shoulder and kissed her forehead and lifted her chin so she looked directly into his eyes.

"We're gonna be okay, Cadie. Do as I say, and we'll get you into the car. Okay?"

Cadie gulped and tried to stop crying. She nodded and said, "I, I'm sorry, I'm so sorry."

David was watching the shepherd as he took the tray off the wheelchair. The dog had stepped forward and waited. When nothing happened, he took two more steps forward. The other dogs were coming up behind him.

David tried to unhook the shoulder straps. One hook was jammed. For a moment he was stymied. Then he looked down. The shears were lying at his feet. He grabbed them and clipped the strap. Cadie was free!

He looked up. The shepherd had moved even closer. He was getting ready to attack. He had to get Cadie into the car fast!

He stood up, bent over, and moved to the rear car door opening. He reached in and grabbed another potted plant. He peeked over the windows. The shepherd was slowly coming closer with other dogs behind him. Suddenly, he stood up and heaved the plant at the shepherd. It landed in front of the shepherd and threw pot pieces and dirt up into the shepherd's face. The shepherd jumped back and retreated across the road. The other dogs were spooked and retreated much further.

David didn't watch the dogs. He slid into the ditch and pulled Cadie from the wheelchair and dragged her up far enough to get a grip on her waist. "Hang on, Cadie!" he yelled as he yanked her up. She threw her arms around his neck and hung on. David suddenly jerked her up, and Cadie was on the road in front of the car door. Hoping she wouldn't be injured, he yanked her up enough to get her through the doorway onto the floor then shoved her in and slammed the door. Cadie was scratched and bruised, but she was in the car now, and the dogs couldn't get to her.

David was climbing into the driver's seat when the shepherd got there. The dog got a mouthful of shirt and pulled him out of the car. All he could think of was keeping the dogs from Cadie. As he fell, he managed to get his hand on the outer door handle. When he hit the ground, he used all his strength to slam the front door. There were so many dogs, a Rottweiler, a terrier, at least ten others, even a chihuahua. He could see them standing back waiting for the shepherd to kill him or get him down flat. Then they would be on him, too.

The shepherd was pulling him face down away from the car into the ditch. David threw his arms out trying to find something to grab onto. His arm was pulled over something hard, a rod or—it was the flashlight! He managed to grab it, twist his body, and aim its high beam at the shepherd's face. Startled, the dog jumped back, letting go of his shirt. David hit the dog's head with the flashlight. The shepherd jerked his head back then lunged forward and sank his teeth into David's back through his shirt. David screamed and dropped the flashlight as the dog dragged him forward and down into the ditch.

David threw his hand over and dragged it trying to get a hold of something, anything. His hand caught the handle of the shovel. He couldn't lift it. He was being dragged over it. Then suddenly it was free. Several of the smaller dogs were getting brave. They nipped at him, making little bites then rushed away. David did his best to shake them off, but they kept coming back. David threw his other hand over and twisted his upper body until both hands were on the shovel. Then he jerked up as hard as he could and lifted the shovel. He brought it down on the shepherd's head. The dog yelped and fell back then crouched in the ravine. He was ready to jump. David sat up and brought the shovel down again, but it hit only the dog's front leg.

The dog yelped and pulled back. Then he crouched, head down and thrust forward, prepared to attack.

David could do no more. He was cut and bleeding everywhere. He couldn't lift the shovel again. He sat staring at the dog. *Cadie is okay*, he thought. *She's okay*.

His body slumped. He saw the shepherd jump toward him as he heard a shot. The shepherd pivoted in mid-air and fell to the ground. Another shot and another. The rest of the pack was yelping and barking.

"David, we're here! The dogs are running away!" Miquel was yelling as he ran to David. "I called the sheriff. He is getting an ambulance for you." Miguel looked down at the empty wheelchair in the ditch. "Oh, David, we are too late for the little girl!"

Jimmy was standing next to Miguel. He covered his face and started crying.

"No," David whispered. "She's okay. She's in the car."

The sheriff called Diane. Diane drove over to the site and was with Cadie and David when the paramedics got them stabilized and into the ambulance. Cadie insisted on riding with David and holding his hand. Diane had to drive behind them. She kept thanking God for this miracle.

At the hospital, they were both treated and released. Because David was bitten by so many different dogs, he would have to go through rabies treatment, which they had already started.

Cadie was covered with bug bites and scratches and scrapes from falling into the ditch and David's rough rescue. Her hair was full of stickers, and one tooth was chipped. Her left wrist was badly bruised.

It was twisted under the tray when the wheelchair turned over.

Along with scratches and scrapes courtesy of the ditch and bushes, David had a sprained ankle and many dog bites. The shepherd bit deeply into his back. The smaller dogs had sneaked in and bit his arms, his legs, his ear, while he was fighting off the shepherd.

Both were covered with bruises, and it was a miracle neither of them had any broken bones.

They couldn't catch the dogs. They had raced into the desert to hide when the cars showed up, and they all got away. But there was a plan to find them before they attacked anyone else. The sheriff said the shepherd was dead, and without the leader, they would be easier to find and catch.

They all rode home in Diane's car. She made lemonade and sandwiches for them then David and Cadie laid down for naps.

When Cadie woke up, she called out in an excited voice, "Mom, it's Christmas Eve! We gotta hurry and get to church!"

Diane ran to Cadie's room, and David woke up, too. He sat up gingerly. His back was bandaged. The dog bites were deep. It was a miracle his spine was all right. He hurt everywhere. He listened as Diane talked to Cadie.

"Cadie," Diane began, "This has been a very difficult day. The doctors said you and David need to rest a lot."

"But, Mom, we'll miss seeing the baby Jesus." Her voice faltered. "This is our first Christmas here, and I spoiled it!"

Cadie started crying.

"Cadie?" David called from the doorway. "You feel good enough to go to church?" He paused. "We look like heck, you know."

Cadie looked down at her soiled, torn clothes and bandaged arms.

"Yeah, I guess I do look kinda beat up." She looked up at David. "You look worse than me!"

She laughed, and David did, too. Then she stopped and said in a serious voice, "But I still want to go. I want us to remember this as a great Christmas." She looked down sadly and said very softly, "Not the Christmas Cadie wrecked!"

Diane patted Cadie on the back. "Honey, we'll make tomorrow the best Christmas ever! But you need to rest now. It's okay, Cadie. Don't …"

David interrupted, "Cadie, if you can get up and go, I will, too."

He hopped over to her bed, making a pained face, then took a deep breath and smiled and stuck out his hand. "Deal?"

Cadie solemnly shook his hand. "Ow!" They both winced.

"Deal!" Cadie shouted, "Let's go!"

Diane looked disbelievingly at the two of them—battered, scraped, in dirty, torn clothes—and threw up her hands.

"Okay," she said, "I give up. There is no sense of reason in this room."

She marched to the doorway, turned around, and said, "Well, if we're going, move it! Let's go!"

"But, Mom, we should change…"

"No time," Diane interrupted. "We go as is. Come on, let's go!"

"But…" David started but stopped when Diane glared.

"Right," David said, bowing his head. "You heard her, Cadie."

Cadie nodded, wide-eyed.

"To the car, David," Diane said as she helped Cadie get into her chair.

"Right," David said. "I'll just go get in the car." He hopped out of the room.

Diane looked at Cadie's solemn face then grinned. "I love you, Cadie. So does David."

"I know, Mom." Cadie smiled. "I know now."

When they got to church, they were greeted by everyone. Part of the rescue was taped and shown on the news, so most people already knew. When the pastor saw them coming in, he stopped the service and ran to greet them.

It was a nice service, hearing the Christmas story, singing carols, and there was a living tableau of the manger scene.

It was late by the time they got home. David hopped to the bedroom and stood nearby while Diane got Cadie into bed. She woke up for just a moment when Diane pulled her covers up and smiled at them, then fell asleep again. David brushed her hair back and kissed her forehead. They were all exhausted and slept late the next morning.

On Christmas morning, Diane brought Cadie a cup of cocoa and sat on the bed while she sipped it. David stood in the doorway.

"Can I sit by David," Cadie asked.

David was very happy she wanted to sit by him, and he was surprised and pleased that he could understand what she said. "Of course," he replied. He felt an overwhelming love for this little girl. Not just liking, but love.

They had breakfast then sat in the living room. Cadie sat in her chair close to David. There weren't many gifts under the scrubby Christmas tree, but it didn't matter. They listened to carols and watched "A Charlie Brown Christmas." They read the Christmas story, and then they opened the gifts.

The last gift was for David. It was a small box with a picture of an angel on all six sides. A ribbon was tied loosely around it, the bow coming undone. It was from Cadie. When he opened it, little pieces of paper spilled out fluttering to the floor. David looked puzzled.

Cadie was grinning. "It's snowing," she said softly, then louder, "You wanted snow. It's snowing!"

David blinked away tears and hugged Cadie, tipping most of the snowflakes out of the box. "It *is* snowing," he laughed.

The phone rang, and Diane went to answer it.

She came back into the room just as the doorbell rang.

"I'll get it," Cadie said. She opened the door then stepped back and said, "David! Mom! Look!"

"Who is it?" David called.

"It's us, sweety."

Diane ran to the door. "Mom? Dad? I can't believe you're here. Come in! Come in!" They came through the door followed by David's parents, George and Joni. "We're here too, Diane."

After many hugs and kisses, Diane's mother explained. 'Cadie called a few days ago to wish us a Merry Christmas." Cadie smiled. "She sounded so sad, and you were so far away, and we missed you so much, we…"

"She ordered last minute tickets over the Internet," interrupted her father.

"And when they told us," continued George, "this new grandma here decided we needed to come too."

"And here we all are!" David's mother was beaming.

"I don't know where … We'll work out sleeping later." Diane laughed looking a bit flustered.

"Don't be silly. We have hotel rooms just a few miles from here. We already dropped off our luggage."

They were all talking at once.

Suddenly, Joni looked closely at David and Cadie. "What in the world happened to you two?"

It took a while to tell the story, and their audience was very attentive. During the telling, Cadie broke in to say, "He saved me! He wasn't even afraid of the dogs!"

"Oh yes I was!" David responded, nodding.

Cadie grabbed his arm and said, "But you didn't run away. You didn't leave me. You saved me."

David smiled at her and said, "I will never leave you, Cadie."

When the story was done, everyone cheered.

George said, "We want to take you out to dinner today for Christmas. That's why we came so early before you started cooking."

David protested, "Dad, I have to work today." Cadie piped in proudly, "At the restaurant."

"What?" David's dad said.

"She said 'at the restaurant.'" Cadie hugged his arm, and David grinned back.

Diane interrupted. "David, that phone call was from Jackson."

She turned to the others and explained, "David's boss."

"He saw you and Cadie on the news. He said you're on paid leave until you're all better. He wants us to come to the restaurant for dinner, or he will bring it here. David, he said he is so proud of you."

Diane smiled, turning to Cadie. "He said you look beautiful on television." Cadie grinned.

They talked for a while, then Joni looked down at the floor and asked, "I've got to ask, what's all this paper on the floor?"

"Snowflakes. Cadie made them for David."

"Oh, how sweet."

They had lunch together sitting wherever they could. There were only four kitchen chairs, so they spilled over into the living room. David's mother sat by Cadie, and they chatted, heads together. *Like conspirators*, David thought. He was amazed that she seemed to understand Cadie so easily. *But I can, too*, he thought. *I can understand her too, now. Not everything yet, but I'll learn.* He grinned.

About one o'clock, the grandparents got ready to return to the hotel. David's mother glanced at Cadie then said, "You know, Diane, we could take Cadie with us, and you could take a nap before dinner. If she wants to, of course. We'll make sure she gets a nap."

Cadie nodded vigorously.

When they all left, Diane decided that was a great idea, set the alarm, and she and David promptly fell asleep. When the alarm went off, she brought a chair for David to sit on to shower, then she showered. They were dressed and ready when the others returned to pick them up.

Cadie came up to the door to get them. "Surprise! It's a surprise!" shouted Cadie. "You have to wear a blindfold."

"What? Well—oh, all right." Joni and George led Diane and David blindfolded to the car.

"Don't look, David! Don't look, Mom!" Cadie was almost screaming with excitement.

Dinner was a grand experience. Jackson was there, and he met and hugged everyone. He sent a bottle of wonderful wine to their table and a Shirley Temple for Cadie. They stayed a long time talking and enjoyed every minute.

When they pulled up to the house, Diane and David were speechless. The outside lights were on, and they could see bits of paper hanging everywhere. On the windows, the doors, the fence posts, the rocks in the yard, even on the big cactus by the corner of the house. Snowflakes. Cadie was clapping her hands in delight. Cadie had the idea, and everyone had helped. The grandparents laughed as they described cutting snowflakes all afternoon. Diane caught a glimpse of Marian and the other neighbors watching from Marian's house. She waved at them, and they waved back. They had all helped with cutting the paper snowflakes and hanging them all around the yard. Cadie had friends.

Diane and David both cried.

It was a happy ending, but the story doesn't end there. That night while they all slept, the temperature dropped, and God sent real, powdery snow to Arizona. David woke Diane, and Diane woke Cadie, and they all went out to play in the snow. Diane laid Cadie in the thin layer of snow, then she helped David lay on one side of Cadie, and she laid on the other side. Then they all made snow angels with their arms. They made a tiny snowman about a foot high on Cadie's tray, then Diane placed him on the biggest rock in the rock bed so the neighbors would see him in the morning. Diane took a dozen or more pictures.

They sat and threw snowballs at each other, and then, too sleepy to do any more, they went back inside and had hot cocoa. Cadie fell asleep with her head resting against David. They pushed her into her bedroom and put her in bed, then took her outer clothes and boots off and tucked her in, and Diane kissed her goodnight then went out to the hall. David lingered by the bed, brushing Cadie's hair back and just looking at her.

Cadie opened her eyes. Her voice was sleepy. "David?"

"Yes."

"Are you my daddy now?"

He looked down at her for a long moment, blinking back tears.

"Oh, yes," he answered, then leaned down and kissed her forehead.

Cadie sighed. Her eyes closed, and she turned on her side. "Goodnight, Daddy," she whispered.

Diane watched from the doorway, smiling. *It's enough*, she thought. Friends, family, and snowflakes. It was enough. It was more than enough.